HOME *on the* RANCH

HER COWBOY HERO

————— ⚹ —————

PAMELA BRITTON

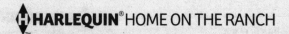

H HARLEQUIN® HOME ON THE RANCH

Recycling programs
for this product may
not exist in your area.

ISBN-13: 978-1-335-83488-1
ISBN-13: 978-1-335-04187-6 (Direct to Consumer edition)

Home on the Ranch: Her Cowboy Hero

www.Harlequin.com

Printed in U.S.A.

"This is your place?"

Colby didn't mean the words as an insult. Her apartment just looked so different than what he'd expected he found himself asking the question, but when he glanced over at her he saw her chin lift.

"It's not much, I know, but at least it's mine. You should try going to school full-time and raising a kid all on your own, because, goodness knows, Paisley's dad refuses to give me a dime for child support."

He stopped the flow of words coming from her mouth by touching her hand.

"I didn't mean it that way."

Didn't he, though? Wasn't that exactly what he'd thought as he pulled up in front of her place?

"You amaze me."

The words were so far from what she'd expected to hear her eyes widened in surprise, or maybe they did so because he'd tugged on her hand, pulling her toward him, and he realized another truth in that moment: he could no more resist her than he could control gravity.

Dear Reader,

Every once in a while you stumble across a place that so inspires you as a writer, you know you want to write about it. That happened to me when I visited a place called Exodus Farms in Anderson, California. I was so inspired by the tales of healing and love, all done with the help of horses, that it brought tears to my eyes.

As luck would have it, I had proposed a book about a therapeutic horse ranch. A long time ago I had fallen in love with a secondary character in *Winning the Rancher's Heart*. Colby Kotch was one of those characters who just screamed wounded hero, and I'd been dying to write about him ever since he'd walked onto the page. Who better to pair him with than Jayden Gillian, the sister of my hero in *Rodeo Legends: Shane*.

I have a confession to make, though. This book gave me fits. Colby is such a tortured hero that I knew it'd take someone special to bring him around. Jayden Gillian might have come across as a pampered princess in previous books, but she's anything but. She has her own crosses to bear. It was a rocky road to get them to talk to one another, but when they finally did, I realized the road to love often starts with two people becoming friends— best friends.

I think this is my fortieth book. (I've honestly lost track. ☺) It's funny because I learn something new with each new story. If you've been with me since the beginning, THANK YOU. And if you're new to my books, you should know that they almost always feature horses, cowboys and a strong-willed heroine—my own personal recipe for fun.

Best,

Pamela

With more than a million books in print, **Pamela Britton** likes to call herself the best-known author nobody's ever heard of. Of course, that changed thanks to a certain licensing agreement with that little racing organization known as NASCAR.

But before the glitz and glamour of NASCAR, Pamela wrote books that were frequently voted the best of the best by the *Detroit Free Press*, Barnes & Noble (two years in a row) and *RT Book Reviews*. She's won numerous awards, including a National Readers' Choice Award and a nomination for the Romance Writers of America Golden Heart® Award.

When not writing books, Pamela is a reporter for a local newspaper. She's also a columnist for the *American Quarter Horse Journal*.

Books by Pamela Britton

Home on the Ranch: Rodeo Legend

Harlequin Western Romance

Rodeo Legends: Shane

Cowboys in Uniform

Her Rodeo Hero
His Rodeo Sweetheart
The Ranger's Rodeo Rebel
Her Cowboy Lawman
Winning the Rancher's Heart

Visit the Author Profile page
at Harlequin.com for more titles.

For Ginger Salido.
Thank you for sharing Exodus Farms with me. This book would not have been the same without you.

Chapter 1

Sometimes, life wasn't fair.

"It's not that you weren't qualified," Patty said. Jayden's friend and mentor sounded as disappointed as she felt. "You had all the right qualifications. You just didn't have the work experience the other candidates had."

Yeah. Experience she couldn't gain because she had a three-year-old daughter to take care of all on her own. Not that she would change being a mom for the world. Paisley was the light of her life, her reason for busting her butt and earning a degree in sports medicine in record time because she'd been determined to prove her dad wrong. The stalemate between them wasn't going to end now, not if she had anything to say about it.

"But I have a bit of good news," Patty went on. "I heard about something at Dark Horse Ranch."

Jayden glanced over at Paisley, her daughter stretched

out on their tiny living room floor, felt-tip pens scattered around, the blooming petals of a flower being drawn in vivid red strokes. She loved to draw, although usually horses. Well, stick horses. She might be three, but her ability to focus always amazed Jayden, although she'd taken to chewing on the end of her thick blond braid lately, something Jayden should probably stop her from doing.

"You know the place, don't you?" Patty asked.

"Not really." She plopped down in a kitchen chair, keeping an eye on Paisley. Darn it. She'd been counting on the job at VDC Sports Therapy. She'd been telling everyone about it, taking pride in the fact that she wouldn't have to move away to find work like so many people had predicted when she'd announced her major in college. Patty had been her ace in the hole. The office manager at VDC and a friend. She'd practically guaranteed her the job.

"I don't think it's far from your dad's place."

Jayden winced at the mention of her father. She'd barely spoken two words to him since he'd basically called her a bad mom right after his heart attack. One would think a near-death experience would soften a man, but not where she was concerned.

What had her friend been saying?

"It's down the road from my dad's place," she said absently. "Next door to Reynolds Ranch."

Everyone in town had heard about the state-of-the-art facility built for veterans with PTSD and other war-related injuries. It had been fully staffed for years. She'd never even thought about looking for work there.

"Anyway," Patty continued, "it's a full-time PT aide position. You'd be working at the ranch. I guess they have a pretty amazing therapy center. Very few veterans at one time, so the workload wouldn't be crazy busy like it would have been here." Patty lowered her voice. "And no whiny old ladies complaining about their hips."

Which was her friend's way of trying to make her feel better. She appreciated the effort even if her mood didn't improve. She'd had to borrow money for last month's rent from her aunt, and she'd hated doing that because all she needed was for her dad to find out about it. He'd made it clear she was on her own, and for the most part she'd done all right. But this past semester she'd had to cut back on her hours at the coffee shop while looking for a job and finishing up some final credits. She hadn't worried about it. She'd been riding on a bubble of optimism. She would finally have her degree. She could find a job that paid enough to support her and Paisley and not have to worry about Paisley's dad, Levi, pitching in to help—which he never did. She'd finally be able to move out of her cheap apartment. She could work for a hospital eventually, pay Aunt Crystal back…

"Are you there?"

Jayden shook her head. "Sorry. I'm just trying to remember if I've ever met the people who own Dark Horse Ranch. I don't think so, but I'm pretty sure my dad knows them."

"If he does, you should ask him to give them a call. I mean, I know the two of you don't talk much anymore, but it wouldn't hurt to ask. We've had dozens of applicants for the job here, Jayden. You'd be surprised. But you were one of our top candidates. If my boss hadn't overruled my choice, you'd be working for us right now, but you should get right on this other job. When word gets out that Dark Horse is hiring…"

It would be a cold day in hell before she asked her dad for help.

Your mother would be so disappointed in you.

The words still had the ability to make her eyes sting.

"Got it." She took a deep breath. She'd ask Uncle Bob to call them. "Thanks for the heads-up, Patty."

"Sorry I couldn't do more, honey."

"It's okay. I understand."

Jayden hung up, trying not to feel too glum. Patty had graduated a year ahead of her, working her way up to manager of VDC in record time. She'd find a job, too, sooner or later.

You're living in squalor when you could be living here at the ranch.

She shook her head. *Stop thinking about it.*

She might not have lived up to her dad's expectations of her—pregnant right out of high school, married and then divorced—but that didn't mean she was a bad mom, which was what he'd implied. Her bitterness turned to resolve.

"To heck with it." She stood up and grabbed her phone. "Paisley, let's go for a ride."

Her daughter looked up at the sound of her name, blue eyes full of curiosity, blond braid dropping over one shoulder. Jayden wasn't usually so impulsive, but she was tired of life handing her lemons when all she wanted to do was make lemonade. She had a free hour or two before work, and she had to drop off Paisley at her aunt's anyway. Aunt Crystal wouldn't mind if she was a little early. And like she'd told Patty, Gillian Ranch was right down the road from Dark Horse Ranch and the home of Hooves for Heroes, so why not take the bull by the horns?

That turned out to be a little harder than she'd thought. An hour later she sat in front of the massive iron gates that led to the therapy center. The granite pillars that held them in place made it seem like an ancient fortress. She couldn't even see the ranch from the road, just grass pastures and tall oaks behind a white fence that stretched to her left and right.

Darn it.

She'd assumed someone would be home, had pressed the call button on the control panel at least a dozen times. Her eyes scanned the back seat via the rearview mirror, looking to see how Paisley was doing before remembering she'd just dropped her off. That was how rattled she was by the day's events.

Okay. Plan B. She checked her cell phone, and when she spotted only a few bars of service, she slipped out of her car. She had to walk a few steps to find a good signal, quickly doing a search for the ranch's name, then dialing the number before she chickened out.

"Dark Horse Ranch," answered a gruff voice that did nothing to calm her nerves.

"Oh, hey, hello." She took a deep breath. The wild oats smelled sweet this time of year, and it was such a familiar scent while growing up that it soothed her nerves. "I was looking for the owner of the ranch." She turned around in place, shielding her eyes against a hot noonday sun.

"Who's calling?" asked the voice in an even lower and more ominous tone.

"I'm actually a neighbor," she said, trying to interject perky friendliness into her words. "I'm Jayden Gillian of Gillian Ranch. Reese Gillian's daughter, and I was hoping to speak to someone about the job you have available for a PT aide."

Silence. Jayden looked around…

And that was when she spotted it. A little black bubble beneath the sign. Security camera. Good Lord. Had he seen her mash all the buttons in a fit of frustration?

"I take it you're the one who's been pressing the call button over and over again?"

She wanted the earth to swallow her up whole. She stared up at the security camera, smiled, waved.

"Well, yes, actually, I was just sort of hoping to speak to someone toda—"

The gates thumped, then groaned and started to open. She didn't know if that was a good thing or bad.

"Follow the signs to the stables," said the voice. "Back of the property. Past the main house."

The line disconnected.

Colby Kotch just shook his head, rolling away from his desk before standing, but not without one last glance at the security screen on his desktop.

She waved one last time.

Like it was no big deal that she was the reason he'd had to run up a flight of stairs and to the office above the covered arena, and all because she wouldn't stop pressing those damn buttons. He headed back downstairs, grumbling to himself the whole way. Name-dropping to get a foot in the door. He had no idea how she'd heard about the job, but he'd listen to her spiel and then send her on her way.

"You get up there in time?" Brennan Connelly asked. Beneath the brim of the man's tan hat, his gold eyes seemed to laugh. Colby had promised to shoe Bren's horse today, something that he rarely did anymore but that he enjoyed doing when time permitted. He always made time for the boss's brother-in-law.

"Barely," Colby said, bending to pick up the bay gelding's foot. "Good thing, too, because I have a feeling the person on the other end would have just called me back."

"Oh?" asked Bren. He stood by the head of his horse, which was cross-tied in a grooming stall along the back wall of a massive covered arena. Next to the open area was a stall, a whole row of them, actually, some horses sticking their heads out to watch him work with Bren's horse, others staring past the wooden rail that ringed the arena in the middle of the building.

Bren patted his horse. "Desperate to get on the waiting list to be a guest?"

"Actually." Colby dug dirt out of the gelding's hoof. "We're hiring a new aide, someone to help pick up the slack. Getting harder and harder to do my physical therapy around here without a little help."

"Oh, yeah." Bren's brows lifted. "Jax told me you've added five more slots for veterans?"

Jaxton Stone was his boss, and the kindest man Colby had ever met. Real salt of the earth. The whole family was great, from Jax's wife, Naomi, to Bren and his wife, Lauren, and all the kids who were usually running around, although some of them, like Bren's stepson, weren't kids anymore. Kyle was a senior in high school now.

"We could have added ten," he said, tipping the hoof left and right, making sure it looked healthy, checking the angles. "This place just gets busier and busier."

"You ready to take on even more vets?" Bren asked. "I see the cabins out front are done."

Colby tucked the hoof pick back in his work apron then picked up the nippers, examining the horse's hoof for another moment before saying, "Ready as I'll ever be. Feel better when we hire some more help. Gonna be crazy busy around here when we open up for the summer season."

"It always is," Bren said.

They usually helped four people at a time, but with the new quarters out back, they'd be ramping things up. That was good. Colby found his job tremendously rewarding, especially when he watched someone walk out of their facility who maybe hadn't been able to do that before their arrival. And if those veterans had PTSD? Well, the horses worked miracles with that type of patient, too.

"Someone coming?" Bren asked, turning to peer down the stable aisle to the opening at the end.

"Yup," he grunted, nipping off a small piece of hoof, concentrating. "The gal who called. She was at the gate."

A few more nips and he was satisfied, dropping the horse's hoof before he slowly stood. He followed the direction of Bren's gaze, watching through the massive opening at the end of the covered arena as a silver car that'd seen better days drove toward them. He tossed the nippers on the ground and wiped his hands on his leather chaps.

"She wanted to introduce herself. Needs a job. Figure I'll let her hand me a résumé and send her on her way." Because he doubted she'd have the qualifications he was looking for. He wouldn't be that lucky.

"That's Jayden Gillian's car," Bren said.

Leave it to the town sheriff to know who everyone was and what car they drove. Course, the Gillians were Via Del Caballo royalty. Jayden's dad was some kind of famous professional cowboy. Her uncle, too. Team ropers. National Finals Rodeo champions numerous times. A couple of their boys had followed in their footsteps. One of them had even won the average last year, the money he'd earned pushing him to the top of the standings and his first world championship. Funny, though, Colby had never heard about a daughter.

"I should probably go meet her," he said, the car disappearing from sight while she parked in front of the stable area. "She sounded like a handful on the phone."

Bren had the most amused expression on his face. "You mean you've never been introduced?"

"Nope."

"And she wants a job?"

"Yup."

Bren laughed. "This ought to be interesting."

"What do you mean?"

Bren tipped his hat back, and his expression could only be called gleeful. "Only that Jayden Gillian isn't the type to take no for an answer, so if your plan is to brush her off, you're in for disappointment."

Just as he'd thought. Spoiled little rancher's daughter. He'd met her type before.

"I think I can handle her."

Bren released something that sounded like a laugh. Colby ignored him and headed for the barn door. Little did Bren know, but he had lots of experience handling willful women. Back in Texas he'd met more than a few, most of them hoping to land the elusive Colby Kotch. Not because they wanted him. Oh, no. They wanted the family fortune. But that was information he'd kept to himself. He'd never told his boss, or anyone in Via Del Caballo, about the family oil business, although it wouldn't surprise Colby if Jax had unearthed the truth. The man made a living as a military contractor, which meant he probably had ten-page dossiers on all of his employees.

He heard a car door slam and wanted to head her off at the pass, which was why he rushed toward the entrance. She must have been rushing, too, which would explain why they nearly collided.

"Whoa there," he said, grabbing her by the shoulders. "You—"

The word *okay* died in his throat.

A pair of the most spectacular blue eyes he'd ever seen had grown wide. Those eyes robbed him of breath in the most bizarre and peculiar way—sort of like he'd been punched in the gut.

"I'm so sorry," she said with a smile, her long black hair swinging out behind her. Black brows and super-dark lashes framed those spectacular eyes. "I'm looking for the owner."

He couldn't think clearly.

"Is he around?" she asked, obviously puzzled by his lack of response. "I think I talked to him on the phone?"

He realized then that he was still holding her, so he quickly stepped back, suddenly able to breathe once he let her go.

Holy crap, what had just happened?

"He told me to come to the barn," she added, looking around and spotting Bren down the barn aisle.

"Oh, hey, Sheriff Connelly."

She smiled, a big, beautiful grin that made his heart

do something weird. It was then and there that Colby realized something. The phrase *breathtakingly beautiful* had a literal meaning.

"I'm him," he managed to gasp out.

"Him who?"

"I manage this place. Well, the therapy program, but I oversee pretty much everything else."

She eyed him up and down, and he saw doubt on her face, probably because he looked more like a farrier in his dirty jeans, leather apron and dusty white T-shirt, all topped off with a straw cowboy hat.

"Colby Kotch," he added.

"Really." She aimed her smile in his direction. "Nice to meet you, then, Colby Kotch. I'm Jayden Gillian."

He wasn't so sure it was nice to meet him, not at all. Bren had been right. Nothing would be easy where Jayden Gillian was concerned, and he had a feeling nothing would ever be the same, either.

Chapter 2

He didn't look happy. Jayden tried not to panic. Darn her impulsiveness. She should have just made an appointment.

"Wow, this place is really something," she said, hoping to charm him out of his bad mood.

"Yes, it is," he said without a change of expression, but the way he drawled his words made her look at him more closely. He sounded like he was from the South.

"I can't believe how big it is."

They stood in front of a huge covered arena, one two stories high and built out of redwood with large wooden beams that reminded her of the ribs of a ship. She'd never seen anything like it, but on the way to the stables, she'd passed a home just as lavish. And then, a few hundred yards across from where she'd parked, matching single-story cabins. Whoever the owner was, he had to have money, because the arena echoed the home's architecture with its glass windows and wood exterior. They stood outside, on the short side; huge doors with glass inlaid into the middle had been slid open, revealing a sand arena inside. Posh.

She took a step back, covered her eyes against the glare of the sun in the cloudless sky. He didn't say anything as she looked up. There were windows along the walls of the second floor, and so she would bet there were apartments or offices or something up there.

"Are there stables along the other side of the arena, too?" she asked, pointing to the row of stalls that lined the right side and where he'd been standing a moment before.

"No, just that one side." She watched him take a deep breath. "We only need a few really great horses for our program."

"And you're expanding?" she asked, because the redwood cabins she'd passed had looked new. They were set into the side of a hill in the same way as the main estate had been, but on a much smaller scale, and the ground around them looked scarred, as if earth had been freshly moved to make way for them.

He nodded, and she tried not to get too excited. That must be why they were hiring. And if they were expanding, that meant a chance for advancement, but only if she could convince them to hire her.

"I'd love a tour."

His left brow twitched. "I'm sure the owner would be happy to show you around when everything's finished."

Brushed off. But she was made of sterner stuff than he probably thought. Her father was the king of poker faces. This man would have to work harder to intimidate her.

"Is it okay if we talk right here, then?" she asked. "Or is there an office or someplace we could meet?"

She realized then that she'd forgotten her résumé in the car. Darn it.

"Right here is fine." He looked down at her empty hands. "Do you have a résumé?"

Was he a mind reader or something? She hid her dismay behind a face of bravado. "I thought we could chat first."

He crossed his arms in front of him, and she had to admit, he didn't look like a therapist. For a minute she wondered if he was joking, if maybe Sheriff Connelly had convinced his horse farrier friend to pretend to be in charge, but if so, who had answered the phone? Nobody other than him and Bren seemed to be around. Should she wait to see if someone else showed up?

"Okay, then," he said in his Southern drawl. "Talk."

It was one of those awkward moments when she wondered what to do. She glanced at the sheriff again. He was too far away for her to read his expression.

"Okay, then." She tipped her chin up. "My name is Jayden Gillian. I just graduated from UC Santa Barbara with a BA in sports medicine. I plan to go for my master's next, although it might take me a while to complete that phase of my education since I plan to work full-time." She debated whether to tell him about Paisley and her daughter's deadbeat dad, but then decided it was none of his business. "This past summer I worked as an intern for a rodeo company, where I worked with injured cowboys for three months. I developed exercises that would aid in their recovery. I followed up with them at the next rodeo, and if I thought something wasn't working, I adjusted their treatment plan."

He didn't say anything, and she grew more and more uncomfortable, and her discomfort wasn't helped by the fact that whoever he was, he looked like he'd stepped out of the pages of some kind of ad campaign for blue jeans and musclemen T-shirts. He had the biceps of a bodybuilder, or someone who spent far too much time in the gym. Good-looking with his silver eyes, scruffy chin and dark hair. All in all, not her type. She preferred men who were less aware of their own handsomeness. She had a feeling this cowboy knew his effect on women.

"This is an aide position," he said. "Sounds like you might be overqualified."

Overqualified? This morning she'd been *under* qualified.

"Since this would be my first real job after college, I doubt it. I'm looking for experience, maybe even room to grow into a PT position at some point in the future. If you're really some kind of manager here, then I'm sure you understand."

"If?" he asked, lifting his right eyebrow up so high that the brim of his cowboy hat went up, too.

"Well, you just sort of look…"

Dang it. She'd blown it again.

He leaned back, unfolded his arms and rested his hands on his hips, peering down at her like the hero of a comic book cover. All he'd need was a cape and a good gust of wind to blow it around. She squirmed beneath his stare.

"…like a horseshoer," she finished.

"Because I am. Sometimes. We all wear a lot of hats around here—"

"I didn't mean—"

He held up a hand. She obediently lapsed into silence.

"I've been with DHR since we opened our doors. I started out as a ranch manger and physical therapist, but these days I just handle therapy and whatever else they need me to do around here from time to time, including shoeing horses sometimes."

Her cheeks began to burn. She wanted to slink back to her car.

"Second of all, I do understand the importance of getting a foot in the door, and I have no doubt you'd be qualified to—" his eyes swept her up and down "—do whatever it is you do, but the work here is hard. It involves working with horses."

"I grew up on a ranch."

He ignored her. "And with men more often than not—"

"So—"

"Hup, hup." He shook a finger at her. "Damaged men, and yes, some women, but mostly men, some of them mentally unstable. Not to sound sexist or anything, but many of them won't want a woman around, especially a pretty young thing like yourself, not when they're at their worst."

Not to sound sexist? That was exactly how he sounded.

"So if you have a résumé, you can hand it off to me. I appreciate you stopping by. I really do." He gave her a smile that didn't quite reach his eyes. "I'll hand off your résumé to my boss, but don't get your hopes up, because I really think he'll want to find someone who could better relate to our clients, maybe ex-military, probably someone who has medical experience."

Don't get your hopes up?

If the man had any idea how hard she'd worked to get

to where she'd gotten in life, he wouldn't say that to her. These past two years had been tough on her. It wasn't just the financial support she'd lost after her big blowout with her dad; it was the emotional side of things, too. She missed family dinners. Missed being able to pop in and see everything without looking over her shoulder for her dad. Darn it, she felt like an intruder when she dropped Paisley off at Gillian Ranch. But she hadn't let any of that stop her from completing her degree. She would not give up on this, either, especially now that he'd mentioned working with horses.

"I have a résumé in my car."

"Great."

Not that he'd look at it. She could tell that he'd dismissed her in the same way some of the older ranchers around here thought a woman couldn't do a man's job. Well, she would just see about that. Sometimes it wasn't what you knew, but who you knew, and she would bet her uncle Bob knew the owner of this place. She just might ask him to make a call on her behalf.

"Thanks," he said when she handed off a folder with all her information in it.

"It was a pleasure meeting you," she lied.

"Same," he said, holding her gaze.

She refused to look away, took pride in the fact that he was the one to break eye contact, turning toward Bren and walking away. Behind him, the sheriff met her gaze. Jayden waved goodbye. He tipped his hat and then, of all things, saluted her.

She saluted him right back.

"*That* didn't look like it went as planned," Bren said with a laugh as, behind him, Jayden's car started up.

He shook his head. "You were right. She won't take no for an answer."

The laugh lines on Bren's face dissolved into contemplation. "Never met a woman as determined as Jayden Gillian. When she sets her mind to do something, she does it."

"I'm surprised someone like her even wants to work."

"What do you mean?"

He shrugged. "Even I've heard of the Gillian family. Seems like a pretty easy life to me."

Bren stared at him for a moment, and he caught a glimpse of something in his eyes, something that looked like surprise, and then amusement.

"Actually, I heard she had a falling-out with her dad. She's been going it alone for a couple years now."

Why did he have a feeling there was more to the story than Bren let on?

"Anyway, might consider giving her a shot. The Gillians pride themselves on being good at things. I'm sure Jayden is no exception."

And so despite his reservations, later that night Colby forced himself to study her résumé. She had a job. Café Express, one of those drive-up shops, a place he'd seen at least a few dozen times on the main drag through town. They sold fancy drinks and pastries and probably paid minimum wage, but she'd worked there enough years that she must have gone to school at the same time. She'd had other jobs, too, during her high school years, he figured, working backward and guessing her age. Definitely not the résumé of someone who lived off family money. Maybe Bren had been right. Maybe she wasn't the spoiled rancher's daughter he'd pegged her to be. She probably knew a thing or two about horses, too. That was a definite plus. As much as he hated to admit it, he doubted they'd find someone as well qualified as Jayden.

In the end, though, he wasn't given a choice about whether or not she'd be suitable for the job. Not long after he set her résumé down, his boss sent him a text message. It was short and to the point.

I hear Jayden Gillian wants a job. Tell her she can start on Monday.

He stared at the message for a long time. Forced to work with her.

He could hardly wait.

Chapter 3

First day at a new job. Jayden thought she might vomit. It didn't help that Paisley had completely melted down when she'd dropped her off at her aunt's, her soft blue eyes pleading with her not to leave, tears tracking down her cheeks. It would only get worse as time went on, which made her wish for the millionth time that Levi played a bigger role in his daughter's life. The man just couldn't be counted on. If she planned on working toward her master's, she better hope she could save up some money thanks to her new job. She couldn't burden Aunt Crystal any more than she already did. She wasn't getting any younger...

Stop.

One thing at a time, though it was hard not to think about what-ifs. If Levi had been half the man she'd thought she'd married, life would have been so much different.

Instead, he'd taken off the moment he'd realized marrying a Gillian didn't mean a free ride. Perish the thought—her dad had expected him to earn his keep. At least he'd signed the divorce papers. Things could be worse.

Her pep talk didn't help allay her fears. When she punched in the code to the gate, her fingers shook. It was early, the sun touching the tips of a dew-soaked lawn so that the grass sparkled as she drove by. She could tell that somewhere off in the distance a hay field had just been cut. It smelled like green tea, or freshly cut alfalfa, one of her most favorite smells in the world. It would be warm later on, something she'd considered when she'd pulled on jeans and a light-blue button-down. Nothing fancy. She had a feeling Colby wouldn't approve of rhinestone-encrusted jeans, and just why she cared so much what he thought was beyond her. The man could go fly a kite, for all she cared.

She had to take a moment to compose herself in her car when she parked outside the arena, but not too long because she would bet the man watched her somehow. When she stepped into the cool morning air, she took a deep breath, hoping against hope she wouldn't have to deal with Colby at all. Her uncle Bob had spoken to the ranch owner, Jax Stone. Maybe he'd be the one to greet her.

Nobody greeted her.

The place seemed deserted, only the horses quietly munching on hay in their stalls stirring. She hadn't been told where to go, just to show up at 8:00 a.m.

So now what?

The sound of hooves on the driveway caught her attention. She turned back toward the entrance just in time to see Colby ride up on a horse, all John Wayne in his white button-down shirt with a crimson wild rag around his throat and a straw hat that rode low on his brow.

"Howdy, partner," she heard herself say, only to wince inwardly because he probably thought she was mimicking his accent or something.

"You're on time."

She waited for him to add something like "Thanks" or "That's great," but instead he sat in the saddle staring down at her. That was when she noticed he held a lead line, and that he led a horse alongside him, a sorrel with a white blaze.

"Did he get loose or something?"

Clearly he didn't follow her meaning, not right away at least, but then he glanced over at the sorrel. He shifted in his saddle in such a way that she wondered if he was embarrassed, like he'd forgotten the horse was there or something.

"Brought him in for you to ride."

Good thing she'd worn jeans and work boots, then. "Okay."

She didn't sound terribly enthusiastic even to her own ears, but not for the reason he probably thought. She hadn't ridden in a while, that was all. Who had time to do that while going to school, raising a kid and working full-time?

"Figure I can watch you tack up, too. Make sure you know what you're doing."

Who was he kidding? This was *all* about making sure she knew what she was doing. Didn't he know who her family was, though? She'd grown up drinking horse milk. Okay. Not really. But rather than intimidate her, her stomach buzzed in anticipation. She'd missed riding ever since her forced exile, although she supposed if she'd really wanted to, one of her brothers or her uncle Bob could have saddled a horse for her.

"Cool." She walked up to him, taking the lead from his hands. "Hey there," she said to the horse, pausing for a moment to stroke the animal's thick blaze. "You're a pretty boy."

She turned back toward the barn, wondering how he planned to watch when he was on a horse. She had her answer a moment later. He'd gone into the covered arena, where he had a perfect view of the grooming stall across a wooden fence that separated the barn aisle from the arena.

"What's his name?"

"Zippy," he answered, lounging in the saddle with a manner of extreme confidence, arm resting across the horn, shoulders slouched. She tried to project the same attitude as she clipped Zippy into cross ties—cotton leads that attached to the horse's halter, one on each side. Then she turned and spied a basket of grooming tools hanging on a post.

He didn't say a word.

If his intention was to intimidate her or make her nervous, then putting her to work with horses had the opposite effect. The nutlike scent of the horse's coat made her inhale deeply, calming her racing heart. When it came time to pick Zippy's feet, she'd forgotten all about Colby standing there, she was so engrossed in her task.

"Saddles are in the room to the left."

She straightened, the blood draining from her head so that she had to rest a hand against the horse's shoulder.

"Okay."

He just stared. Suffice it to say, her first impression of him hadn't improved much with time. He was like some kind of lord and commander sitting there on his horse, reins slack, legs relaxed. Like the picture of Ulysses S. Grant she used to study in her favorite horse book, the one about famous equines throughout history.

She found the saddle right where he said, in a beautiful tack room that would rival the one in the stables back home. Saddles sat on racks along the perimeter of the wall to her left. Bridles rested on horseshoe hooks on the back wall. Cabinets were on her right where she would bet sat a whole host of vet supplies.

It took a moment to choose one of the saddles that looked about her size. She picked a saddle pad from a heap of them atop a wooden rack. She examined the bridles, made her choice and slid it up onto her shoulder.

"I picked a bridle with a snaffle," she said, emerging from the tack room. "That okay?"

"Fine," he drawled softly.

She juggled the saddle, the pad and the bridle, grateful when she could set it all down along the groom stall wall. Damn things were heavy. She'd always grumbled that western saddles were made by men. If they were made by women, they'd be twenty pounds lighter and half the size.

"Okay, buddy. Here we go." She tossed the pad onto the horse's back, moving it forward slightly. Zippy didn't move. She patted his sorrel coat. The saddle came next, and it was even heavier to lift than she'd anticipated. Or maybe she'd just been spending too much time in a classroom and at work. She somehow managed to get the job done, adjusting the stirrups after securing the girth. Zippy took the bridle easily, too.

"What a good boy," she murmured, sliding the leather reins over the horse's ears, all of it coming back to her like it'd been yesterday. She had to adjust the cheek pieces a little, but all in all, she'd gotten the job done in what she knew was a reasonable amount of time.

"Where to?" she asked.

He held her gaze for a moment. "In here." He straightened up. "Safest place to test your abilities."

Like she might fall off or something. Ha. Little did he know. She'd grown up on the back of a horse. She'd even tried jumping for a bit. She was, in her dad's words, an expert equestrienne. That was high praise indeed coming from a man who'd won more team roping world championships than any other cowboy.

And you miss him.

Yes, she silently told herself, she did miss her dad. But he would need to apologize to her before she'd return to the family fold. That would never happen.

She led Zippy into the covered arena, the absence of sunlight chilling the air and making her shiver. Zippy seemed like a sweet old horse. When she stopped just inside the gate, he didn't try to turn around and go back to his stall like a lot of horses would do. He stood quietly while she mounted, too, flecks of dust floating in the air through a beam of light.

"What do you want me to do?" she asked, picking up her reins.

"Just trot around at first." He turned his horse to face her. "You can do more if you feel like it."

"Okay. As long as you realize it's been years since I've been on a horse."

"I don't care." It was like he'd used an eraser to wipe the expressions off his face. He sat there staring across at her. "I want to get a feel for how you ride."

No encouraging smile. No nod of support. No nothing.

"Here we go," she muttered, squeezing the horse forward.

She quickly realized that if horses were cars, Zippy would be a Ferrari. She barely had to do anything to get him to go. And she needn't have worried about the passage of time, because it was like riding a bike. Staying centered over the horse's back came naturally. When she pulled on her right rein, Zippy immediately turned that direction, head down, softly flexing his neck. She pulled him left next. Same response.

"Was he a show horse or something?" she asked, loosening her hips so she didn't bounce as badly. When she glanced at Colby, she could see surprise in his face.

"He was."

"Groovy." She pulled the horse to a stop, then gave the cue to lope, Zippy instantly responding, Jayden laughing because it felt so damn good to ride again. Zippy was a dream. So smooth, even when she got him to run a little faster, doing a figure eight in front of Colby, asking for a lead change and getting one instantly.

"He's amazing," she said, pulling him to a stop in the middle and, just for grins and giggles, asking him to turn on the hindquarters. He spun around so fast it reminded her of her dad's cutting horses.

"That's enough."

When she spotted the look on his face, she had to resist the urge to laugh. It was the same expression she'd seen on her professor's face when she'd recited all the bones in a human hand without missing a beat. She clucked Zippy forward, coming to a stop alongside him.

"That was fun."

"Where'd you learn how to ride like that?"

"I showed cutting horses when I was younger, then

switched to jumping when chasing cows grew too boring. I gave it all up when I—" She almost said "Got pregnant," called the words back just in the nick of time. "Started college," she improvised, which was close to the truth. He didn't need to know her pregnancy came first.

"You're good."

He said it like an accusation. Like she should have told him she knew how to ride.

"I should hope so," she said, patting Zippy on the neck. "I've been riding my whole life."

They lapsed into silence. Up in the rafters she could hear a pigeon coo, then the soft rustle of feathers. A horse nickered in the distance.

"Look." She straightened in the saddle, lifted her chin. "I know I'm not exactly what you were looking for in an assistant, but I'm a hard worker. I'm not afraid to dive in and do what needs to be done. And I take criticism well, so if I do something wrong, just tell me. I promise not to get in your way."

The man was into long, unblinking stares. She could tell it would drive her nuts. She tried to do the same right back and just couldn't. The smile slipped on her face without her bidding. That was her personality. Smile through the tough times.

"Just do your job."

Chapter 4

He was grumpy, he admitted, un-tacking Ranger a half hour later. Not even putting Ranger through his paces had eased the tension in his shoulders. It wasn't her fault she reminded him of his past, and that there were a million things he had to do before their first guest arrived in a week.

"Who do you want me to ride next?" she asked, motioning toward the arena.

That was part of the job sometimes—exercising the horses and taking care of the ranch. Their ranch manager, Derrick, always left this time of year to go visit family. If he were honest, though, it was a huge relief to know she could ride. That'd be a big help until Derrick came back.

"You done already?"

She nodded, stopping in front of the groom stall. He felt his brows lift toward the rim of his cowboy hat. There was a hint of something in her eyes, a twinkle that reminded him of a young colt just before it bolted away from him.

"I'll show you in just a second."

"Need help?" she asked.

He shot her a sideways look of impatience, counseled himself to take it easy on her again. "No, thanks."

She stood there and watched him un-tack, and suddenly he felt like the one on trial. He fumbled the leather girth strap that looped around the rigging ring, his fingers suddenly clumsy, his cheeks blazing beneath his hat. Damn it. What was with him today?

"There's a soda machine at the end of the aisle. Help yourself."

He hoped she'd take him up on the suggestion and give him a bit of breathing room. He frowned, pulling the cinch strap free. He didn't like how edgy she made him feel.

"That's okay."

He glanced over at her. She smiled, her blue eyes as bright as the hottest part of the flame of his welding torch.

"I don't drink soda."

"No?" he muttered, pulling the saddle from Ranger's back. "Good for you."

And there he went again, sounding as cross as his old man. That was why he'd moved away from Cardiff, Texas. Well, one of many reasons. He didn't want to turn out to be like his dad, more concerned with his own selfish desires than his family. He'd thought he'd gotten away from all that when he'd joined the military. Had been proud of the life he'd carved out for himself, but then it'd all come to a screeching end.

"I can take the bridle." She held out her hand.

He stared down at it for a moment, the saddle heavy in his arms, the bridle around the horn dragging on the ground. He'd forgotten he'd hooked the bridle on the damn thing. Something red caught his eye. It was on the back of her hand.

"What's the matter? Couldn't afford a tattoo?" He eyed the flower she'd drawn.

She snatched her hand away so quickly it gave him pause; so did the way she hid her eyes from him, her lashes sweeping down and covering the brief glimpse of— Was it guilt?

"I was just doodling." She shrugged.

He hefted the saddle again, forced himself to look away before he headed toward the tack room. The reins got caught up in his legs and he damn near tripped.

"Do me a favor and put my horse back, would you?" he called over his shoulder.

"Sure."

He heard the thud of the cross ties hitting the groom stall wall. Thank God she was leading Ranger through the stables toward his stall. He didn't like having a damn human shadow. He wondered for a moment about what he'd seen in her gaze just before she'd shielded her eyes, but whatever it was, it was gone when she returned to the tack room.

"Is he yours?"

Took him a moment to figure out what she meant. "You mean Ranger?"

She nodded. "He's gorgeous."

"He belongs to the ranch." He rested his hands on the saddle he'd just set on the saddle rack. "Listen. It'd be a big help if you started mucking stalls." Liar. It'd be better if she kept riding, but for some reason, he didn't want her to do that. "When you're finished, I'll give you a tour of the whole place."

"Sure," she said. "Where do you keep the rakes and stuff?"

"End of the barn aisle."

And she was off. Liz would never have complied so easily. She'd have complained first and then batted those thick lashes.

And now he was thinking about his damn ex.

It'd been years since he'd thought about Liz, the woman who'd capped off one of the worst years of his life by driving a stake through the heart of the Kotch family. He refused to think about her now.

When he walked out of the tack room on his way to fetch another horse, Jayden was already pushing a wheelbarrow with a rake inside it. She didn't seem the least bit cowed by the menial task he'd just assigned her, either.

"Where should I dump the stuff when I'm finished?"

There was warmth and light in Jayden's blue eyes. It lit her up from inside, making it hard to look away from her.

"There's a big pile out back." He took a deep breath, pulled himself together. "We have a guy come in and pick it up once a week. Some kind of organic farmer or something. Just dump it on top."

"Alrighty, then." The words were almost a chirp, a cheerful warbling of her contentment with her lot in life. She didn't seem to mind hard work. He'd give her that much.

He went to go get the next horse to ride before he could think too much about that. She was still hard at work when he peeked in on her an hour or so later.

"When you're done, come upstairs. You'll need to

fill out some paperwork." He tried to sound friendlier. He'd have to try to make this work, at least for now. "I'll show you around afterward."

She leaned up against her rake. "That'd be great."

He scanned the stall she'd been cleaning, pleased by the job she'd done. But it remained to be seen if she could do the most important component of her new job—handle their patients. He hadn't been kidding when he'd told her some of them could be difficult. There were days when even he wanted to give up on some of them.

He heard her climbing the stairs to the second floor, glanced at the time and noted she'd taken less than an hour to clean the dozen stalls. He would add "efficient" to her list of attributes so far.

"Wow," he heard her say from the other side of the glass doors. She'd turned to stare out the windows to her right. He'd done the same thing the first time he'd arrived and climbed the steps, simply gazing out at the view. Rolling hills led to taller, more rocky mountains in the distance. This part of Southern California had a steady stream of moisture thanks to the ocean less than a half hour away. It wasn't that it rained a lot, just that the dew point was high. That meant lush green fields for a large part of the year and pastures dotted with majestic valley oaks.

"Come on in," he called.

She turned, smiled, and with the left half of her face in shadow, she reminded him of the ads he'd seen in his mom's fashion magazines. Beauty in sepia. He had to look away because it still hurt to think about his mom.

"Nice digs," she said, sitting down in front of his desk.

"Here's the paperwork." He slid her a packet of forms,

knowing he sounded terse, angry with his inability to corral his wayward thoughts. He needed to stop kidding himself. The woman was gorgeous. It was hard not to stare at the luminosity of her eyes. They were like glass, they were such a crystalline blue. Add her thick black hair and her heart-shaped face, and she made him feel like a fumble-fingered boy. *That* was what had him so uptight. It wasn't that he gave a fig about having to hire her. It was the damn sizzling attraction he'd felt from the moment he'd first met her.

"Can I bring these back to you later?" she asked.

"Sure," he said, seizing on the excuse to get her out of his office. But wait. Damn it. He'd offered to give her a tour. "Just leave them there while I show you around."

She had a face that showed her every emotion, as if she laid it all out there for everyone to see. It allowed him to read her expression so easily it felt somehow wrong. Right now her face and eyes told him she'd rather not spend any more time with him than absolutely necessary.

He knew how she felt.

"I can exercise more horses if you want."

Her words made him feel even more of a heel. "That's actually my job." She had looked away, and he could tell she held on to her patience by a thread. She wasn't angry. He tried to put a name to whatever emotion flitted through her eyes.

"It's not that I can't use the help." He forced himself to smile, and he watched as her face dissolved into relief. "We had to buy some more horses, and I'm still trying to figure out which ones will work for our program and which ones won't. And our ranch manager is on vacation. He's usually the one in charge of care and maintenance of the place, so I really could use your help until Derrick gets back."

"Well, when you're ready, I'd love to take some of the load off of you there."

She meant it. He could see the sincerity in her gorgeous eyes, and it sealed the realization that he'd made a huge mistake where she was concerned. She was not some spoiled rancher's daughter. Far from it.

"When you do ride, I'd feel better if I was there to share the horses' quirks."

"Smart thinking." She smiled, too, but he would bet hers wasn't forced. "You never know with horses."

Funny, he'd forgotten for a moment that she came from a famous rodeo family, one that lived nearby. That meant the view outside had to be familiar to her, too, and yet she'd still paused for a moment to take it all in, and in her gaze he could have sworn he'd seen sadness.

"How big is the upstairs?"

She'd pulled her hair back into a ponytail, and he found himself wondering if she'd had it professionally dyed. It was so dark that it looked almost purple with sunlight pouring onto it from one side.

"About thirty thousand square feet."

She wore her surprise like a child who'd just been told she lived in a castle. "That's a lot of room."

He shrugged. "Not really. We have to split it between office space, guest quarters and my apartment. I live right next door to the office here." He motioned toward the wall behind him. "And we have a laundry, a kitchen and a community room around the corner. Some of our veterans are in no shape to cook. You'll meet Patsy, our chef, when the vets start arriving."

"Sounds like the owner has spared no expense."

"Money is no object where Jaxton Stone is concerned. He even put in an elevator in the back corner of the arena, just so people with wheelchairs could access the second floor. That was a big problem before. Jax will do almost anything to help the veterans. Therapy. Fitness training. You name it. You should see our new PT room."

He led her toward the landing outside the office. A T-shaped hallway bisected the upper floor. His office sat on the right side at the top of the T, his apartment on the left. Guest quarters and the other rooms were off the center length.

"Let me show you one of the apartments." His keys echoed down the long hall, and his damn fingers refused to cooperate. When he finally managed to swing the door wide, she looked dazed as she walked inside.

"My goodness."

The rectangular room had been designed to maximize the space. The bedroom was behind the wall on their right, closet to his left and a sitting area straight ahead. The back of the couch faced them, the front facing a row of windows. A gas stove sat in the right-side corner so it would serve both the sitting area and the bedroom.

"Are they all like this?"

"The footprints change, but yes." He led her back outside, uncomfortable with just the two of them in the room together. "One of the reasons we built new guest cabins is to more easily accommodate those with severe handicaps. The elevator helps, but it was kind of a pain to have to go all the way around back to get to their rooms. I lived in fear of the thing breaking and someone getting stuck. Not anymore. Now we'll let those with severe disabilities stay in the new cabins, and we won't be limited with how many we can accept. We could really make a difference with some true heroes."

She stared at him strangely, and he tried to understand what he saw on her face. It was as if she'd spotted a curiosity, something that surprised her and intrigued her at the same time. Something inside *him*.

"You really care, don't you?"

He wondered if he should be offended by her words, admitted it shouldn't matter one way or the other and then settled on a shrug. He did care, though, but for reasons she would never suspect.

"They're heroes, each and every one of them, men and women who've made the ultimate sacrifice. It's my job to get them better, both mentally and physically."

Her face seemed to gentle. He saw her begin to smile, found himself fascinated by how it transformed her face.

"Amazing," he heard her murmur.

"What is?"

"This place. You. That I knew nothing about what you did here. I'm blown away."

He shrugged again.

Genuine.

That was the best way to describe her. As open as the Bible that had sat next to his bed the entire time he'd been deployed. And there she went making him think about his past again and memories best left behind, which was why he found himself heading for the exit.

"Let's get the rest of the barn chores done."

Chapter 5

People always claimed horseback riding wasn't really exercise. *Ha.* A week after starting her new job, she still couldn't walk right.

"You ready for today?" He tossed the brush he held back into the groom box on the wall. The horse he was about to ride, Dover, danced in the cross ties, the sound of her hooves muted by the rubber mat she stood upon.

"As ready as I'll ever be."

Because today was the day. Instead of learning her way around the place, cleaning stalls and helping to ride horses, she'd get to greet their new guests. Well, one of them. Everyone else, including the ranch manager, would be arriving over the next week. Colby had told her yesterday they had a guest coming in early—the man was a friend of a friend or something, some kind of special exception.

"I've put the schedule up on the whiteboard."

Tacked to the wooden walls was a board with a grid of names along the left side. He'd written one name down. Bryan Vance. Their new guest. Beneath the column "Check-in" was her name. She'd known that would be her job. Colby had filled her in on the protocol. Once all the other guests started arriving, the veterans would work with one or both of them, aided by a slew of volunteers. Some days veterans would start out riding. Other days it would be weight training. Some days it would just be grooming the horses. She'd been warned it would be slow going at first because the veterans didn't arrive all at once. That suited her just fine. They would ramp up slowly, Derrick returning next week, a cook coming in to care for their guests and staff. Free lunches. Another perk of the job. Thank God, too, because she hadn't had time to pack a lunch this morning. She'd woken up late. And then Levi, who had agreed to look after his daughter for once, had been late to pick up Paisley, forcing her to race down back roads like some kind of stock-car driver. Her hands still shook from the stress of it all.

"Anything special you need me to do before I get started mucking stalls?"

The black gelding he groomed pricked his ears as she approached.

"Just the usual until Bryan arrives."

But she'd only taken two steps toward the wheelbarrow when the familiar sound of an ATV drew her up short. She glanced at Colby. He stared past her.

"Boss man."

That had her spinning around. Her uncle spoke highly of Jaxton Stone, the owner of Dark Horse Ranch. A moment later, when he came into view sitting behind the wheel of a fancy all-terrain vehicle with more chrome than a sixteen-year-old's hot rod, his friendly wave soothed her nerves.

"You guys are getting an early start," he called down the aisle.

Even though she knew her jeans were clean, she wiped them off. Her welcoming grin froze, however, when a light brown bundle of fur came around the corner. It headed straight for her.

"Tramp, no!" her boss called.

"Crap," she thought she heard Colby drawl.

Jayden knew she was the target. She held out a hand, hoping to stave off the canine battering ram. Didn't work. He hit her with the full force of his front paws, and even though it all happened in an instant, she had time to mourn the fact that she was about to fall flat on her bum in front of her new boss.

Only she didn't. Somehow Colby kept her upright.

"Sit," he ordered the dog, pulling her up against him. Her backside connected with his front.

And good Lord, it felt like he wore one of those Hollywood superhero suits, the kind made out of plastic and with sculpted abs that everyone knew no real actor actually possessed. Only Colby's were real. Her damn cheeks reacted instantly. Heck, her whole dang body reacted. Did he spot the bloom of color on her face? Her dad said her cheeks were like a neon sign. One tug of embarrassment and she lit up the whole room.

"That darn dog." Her boss grabbed the animal by the collar. "After all these years you'd think he'd learn not to jump up on people."

"I think training him is a lost cause." Colby gently released her. She couldn't look at him. She didn't want to see the amusement in his gaze. Or the censure. Or whatever reaction he might emote thanks to her clumsiness.

Her gaze locked on his lips.

She darn near jumped back. Why had she done that? Had he noticed her staring at his mouth? If she'd been the color of an Open sign before, she was now the same shade as molten lava.

"It's okay." She forced a smile in the general direction of her new boss. "I'm a klutz."

"No. My dog is a brat."

He said the words with a smile. Jaxton Stone's gaze scanned her. She had a feeling he'd taken her measure the moment he'd clapped eyes on her, and that whatever his first impression was, he would rarely get it wrong. He must have approved of what he saw, because the smile turned into one of welcome.

"I don't mind dogs." She knelt down. Tramp didn't hesitate to approach again, but he'd been suitably cowed, his head lowered, his tail wagging, ears slicked back. His fur was like silk wires, light brown in color, and it stuck out above his eyes like brows.

"You're a silly one, aren't you?" She scratched his head. He looked like a Scottish terrier, only much bigger. The size of a border collie. "I bet you're good at giving kisses."

As if he understood her words, he darted forward, sliding his tongue across her cheek, Jayden drawing back in surprise.

"Thanks." She stood again. "I think."

"He likes you." Jax nodded in approval.

"He probably likes everyone."

"He does," Colby said with the enthusiasm of a man whose patience was tested on a daily basis.

"Nice to meet you, sir." She held out her hand.

"Call me Jax." He went back to studying her again. He wore a white polo shirt and jeans, and his casual attire set her instantly at ease. "You don't look a thing like your dad."

The comment took her aback. No, she didn't, and the mention of her dad made her instantly sad. She looked like her mom, and that sent another pang of sadness through her. Her mom's death had left a huge hole in her sixteen-year-old heart. If she'd been alive she would have seen right through Levi. She would have told her to give the man a wide berth. Instead she'd fallen right into his arms after her mother's death. In hindsight she wondered if Levi had capitalized on her grief. She wouldn't put it past him.

So she took a deep breath, made sure she brightened the wattage of her smile and said, "I take after my mom."

"I don't think I've ever met her before."

Another deep breath. "She died before you moved here."

Jax's eyes filled with so much instantaneous compassion that she wanted to hug him. "I'm so sorry for your loss."

"Thanks."

Jax glanced at her coworker. "Colby tells me you've done a great job so far."

She couldn't keep the surprise off her face. "I hope so."

Tramp had settled down at her feet, the dog never taking his eyes off her, a look of canine adoration on his face as he stared up at her. She couldn't help but smile down at him.

"Listen," Jax said. "The reason I came down early is to give you a heads-up about Bryan. We served together back in the day. He stayed in and I got out. Bryan's a good guy, but I guess he's really struggling." He shook his head. "His sister called me and begged us to take him sooner rather than later. I guess she's worried about him doing something…" He couldn't say the words, but they all knew what he was thinking. "But that's why we started Hooves for Heroes, right?"

A look passed between Jax and Colby, one she didn't entirely understand, but that seemed loaded with subtext. She wondered about it, but then Jax said, "I'm sorry about the extra work it means, what with Derrick still on vacation, but I felt we didn't have a choice."

"Don't worry about it," Colby said. "We'll manage."

"Good." Jax nodded. "I'm going to let you two greet him when he arrives, give him a few hours to settle in before we have a little heart-to-heart." He smiled at them both.

"Colby has me down as the welcoming committee." Jayden glanced at Colby, wondering why he seemed so quiet all of a sudden. Then again, he was always a man of few words. "I have some experience with depression. When my mom died it was tough on me. I know being wounded in battle is nothing like losing a loved one, but I'd be honored to help your friend in any way I can."

Her boss's blue eyes softened just before they filled with approval. "You're right. It's nothing like losing a loved one, but compassion will serve you well in this business." His gaze landed on Colby for a second before shifting back to her. "I presume Colby's showed you how to check in a guest? It's pretty simple. Afterward, you can give Bryan a tour of the place. He can start his first therapy session tomorrow. When do the other veterans arrive, Colby?"

"They'll be dribbling in starting next week."

"Good. Less of a rush that way." He straightened. "Okay, then. Jayden, you should come up to the house on your way home. I'll introduce you to my wife and kids and our other four-legged child, Thor."

"I'd like that."

Her new boss waved as he left. Tramp rode shotgun, and the sight of the dog sitting there like a human passenger made her smile. For the first time since coming to work at Dark Horse Ranch, she felt completely at ease.

"How long ago did your mom die?"

The question surprised her. She took a deep breath before facing Colby.

"Four years ago."

But it seemed like yesterday, although she felt the loss most when she was around Paisley. It didn't seem right that her daughter had to miss out on her grandmother's love. Thank goodness for Aunt Crystal. She didn't know what she'd do without her.

"My mom died, too."

He eyed her in the same way as Jax, in a way that made her feel exposed and vulnerable, but there was something else in his eyes, something that made her heart thump in an altogether new and different way, one that reminded her of when she'd landed in his arms.

"I'm sorry."

Who was this man? she wondered. He seemed such a contradiction at times. Stern and demanding when it came to working with him, yet soft and kind when handling the horses he so clearly loved. And the look he'd exchanged with Jax… It led her to believe this wasn't just a job to him. This was personal.

"Let me get you the forms Bryan will have to sign when he arrives."

He turned away quickly, as if he wanted to escape.

Colby watched her from a window upstairs, the one at the end of the long hall. A small white van pulled in front of the barn. Jayden rushed outside, her black ponytail catching the light as it swung back and forth. He couldn't see her face, but he would bet there was a smile on it. There almost always was. She spoke to the driver first through the passenger window, Colby having to squint against the glare of the sun on the white paint job. With a wave, she moved to the side of the van and the door he knew would be opened for Bryan Vance.

He turned away before they spotted him standing there.

He liked her. He hadn't expected that.

Who was he kidding?

He'd faced the inconvenience of an unwanted attraction all damn week. He found the way her eyes lit up when she smiled completely endearing. She'd been nearly knocked down by Tramp, and the moment he'd touched her, he'd wanted to keep on holding her. Stupid and ridiculous. He'd kept women at arm's length since he'd moved to Via Del Caballo. He didn't plan on that changing anytime soon.

Bzzz.

That damn buzzer. The bane of his existence. Between visiting family members, deliveries and the occasional neighbor looking for a job, he'd be kept on his toes in the coming week.

Bzz. Bzz. Bzz.

"Keep your hat on," he muttered, dashing back to his office. A beat-up old truck sat by the intercom. No idea who it was.

"Yes?" he said into a speakerphone.

"I need to see Jayden."

He switched cameras. A face that seemed elongated thanks to the tiny lens refracting the image stared back at him. A cowboy in black and white.

"Will she know what this is about?"

"Yeah. Tell her she needs to take Paisley for the day. I have someplace to be."

She needed to take *who*? He looked past the guy, spying a kid in a car seat strapped to the bucket seat.

She has a kid?

"I'll tell her you're here." He pressed the button to open the gate. "Drive past the house and to the covered arena in the back. Just follow the road."

Married?

The chair creaked from his weight. He hadn't seen a ring on her finger. Had just assumed...

He caught her walking alongside their new guest. She wasn't exactly pushing the wheelchair Bryan Vance sat in, but she was near him. No fancy electric wheelchair for Sergeant Vance. The burly brown-haired, brown-eyed man pushed the wheels with his hands, the tires crunching on the gravel as the chair rolled along the road that separated the new cabins from the covered arena. She caught his gaze, her black brow lifting in curiosity, but then the sound of a vehicle must have caught her attention because she turned slightly. Any chance he had of warning her went right out the door. She jerked upright.

"You've got a guest." He stated the obvious as he approached. But then he caught sight of Bryan, shocked at how haggard he appeared, as if he hadn't slept in weeks, maybe months. He tried to hide his reaction as he faced the man. "I'm Colby Kotch, and I'll be your therapist."

He wouldn't call the look on their new guest's face a greeting, more like an acknowledgment of his presence. He seemed older than his file had indicated, although maybe that was the gray in his short-cropped brown hair.

"Bryan Vance."

That was all he said. Didn't reach out to shake his hand. Didn't do anything other than spin his chair toward the truck that approached. The skin on his hands was a mix of pink and white flesh. Scars. Probably burns from the IED, and for a moment Colby flashed back to the moment that had changed his life forever. The explosion. The screams of his men…

"What the—"

Jayden's words made him start. He opened his eyes to see Bryan staring at him curiously.

"I think that's my ex."

Ex. Not married. Not that it mattered.

"He said something about dropping Paisley off," Colby explained.

"What?"

She charged toward the moving truck. She reminded him of a soldier in a battlefield. No fear. Shoulders square. Hands clenched to the point that blood leached from her fingers.

"This ought to be interesting."

Colby glanced down at their new guest, privately agreeing. He should move the man along, continue where Jayden had left off. Instead he found himself curiously held in place.

"I can't believe… That no-good, sorry son of a—" She placed her hands on her hips.

The driver's-side door swung open; a lanky man with patchy-looking blond sideburns got out. He slapped a tan cowboy hat on his head.

"What are *you* doing here?"

The man was all cool cockiness in his store-bought tattered jeans and purple paisley shirt. Colby disliked him on sight.

"I can't watch her anymore." He pushed the hat down low. "Got a call from Dusty. He's up at Redding this weekend. Told him I'd go up early and pull slack when he rode."

Jayden seemed incapable of speech for a moment. "You're going to a rodeo a week early to help your friend ride a bull?"

The man splayed his hands. "I told you I might have to leave. You can't expect me to drop everything and watch Paisley all the time."

He could practically hear Jayden count to ten. Her hands clenched and unclenched in time with the unspoken numbers. She glanced toward the truck, where he could see a little girl strapped in a car seat.

"Yes, I can." Her words were far more civil than her body language implied, probably for the little girl's sake. "It's called parenting. She's your *daughter*. And I'm *working*, which is way more than I can say for you."

"I might work, too. I'm on the wait list for Redding. Someone might draw out."

Ah. A rough stock rider. That explained a lot.

She snorted. At least, that was what it sounded like.

The man ignored her, sauntering like a star quarterback over to the passenger-side door.

"You can't leave her here."

"I have to." The man emerged with a little girl in his arms, one with the same blond hair and blue eyes as her dad. "Take her to your aunt Crystal or somethin'. I'm out of here."

"Mama?" the little girl said, a smile bursting onto her face when she spotted Jayden, and then, "Mommy!"

Paisley squirmed like a puppy. The man seemed only too happy to set her down. She ran—well, toddled—to her mom, who scooped her up and held her close.

"I can't believe you're doing this, Levi."

Levi hooked his thumbs in his belt loops and smiled, and something about the way he did it made Colby think he used the grin a lot. Here was a man who knew his effect on women and wasn't afraid to use it.

"She's looking forward to spending time with you."

"Oh? Did she tell you that?"

Levi ignored her. "I'll see you next week, Goldy," he said to his little girl, leaning in, but he didn't close the distance to touch her or kiss her goodbye. "Daddy has to go off and make some money."

"Ha," Jayden huffed.

The man straightened again. "Don't get snarky."

"Just go." Jayden shifted Paisley to the other hip.

The man didn't need to be told twice. He sauntered back around the beat-up old truck and hopped in. Exhaust clouded the air. Jayden stepped back and watched him drive away.

"Something tells me you'll be my tour guide today."

Colby glanced down at Bryan. He had a feeling the man was right. "You mind if we postpone it a little bit?"

"It's your call." His words were coated with a Southern accent laced with the same sugar as a beignet. "My sister's the one paying for this whole ridiculous thing."

Oh, yeah. They would have their work cut out for them with Bryan, but that would have to wait for later. Right now Jayden was walking toward him, her little girl in her arms, tears of frustration in her eyes.

Damn.

He'd never been proof against a woman in tears.

Chapter 6

"I'm so sorry." Jayden pulled Paisley closer, almost afraid to look Colby in the eyes. Behind him, she saw Bryan roll his way toward his cabin. "I can't believe this happened. I'll call my aunt Crystal right now. I just need to go get my cell phone."

"Use the ranch phone." He pointed to the barn wall behind her. She tried not to wince at the look on his face. He was *not* happy.

"C'mon, Pais. Let's go call Aunt Crystal."

She wasn't home.

Colby still stood where she'd left him, in the middle of that aisle, hands on his hips. He wore the same straw cowboy hat he always did, but she would swear he'd pulled it down low on his brow, like some kind of cowboy in an old Hollywood Western.

"I had to leave a message," she confessed.

"I heard."

Paisley wiggled in her arms. "Horse," she announced.

"Yes, they are, baby. But they're not ours." It was like trying to hold on to a wet seal. Once Paisley got an idea in her head, it was impossible to stop her, and today was no exception. She'd spotted her favorite animal in the whole wide world and she wanted down. Now.

"Paisley, stop."

"She can pet them if she wants."

It was either drop her or let her down, so she set her on her feet, but Paisley slipped from her grasp before she could grab her hand.

"Horse." She headed straight for the bay mare in the first stall.

Colby swooped her up as she passed, swinging her around as though he'd done it a million times before. Paisley loved it, giggling.

"Whoa there, little one," he said, smiling as he turned her around to face him, settling her on his hip with an ease that spoke of lots of experience with kids. How strange. She'd never thought of him as a family man.

"Horse." She reached her hand toward the animal in question.

"She loves them. Always has. I wish…"

She shook her head. This was no time to think about her dad and how he'd been the one to teach her to ride and how Reese Gillian hadn't seen Paisley since she was an infant. Aunt Crystal said he never came up to the house when she was babysitting. It broke her heart.

"You wish what?" Colby said.

"Nothing." She forced a smile. "I'm so sorry." She held her arms out, prepared to take her daughter off his hands. "Paisley, come here."

"No, it's okay." He turned toward the first stall on the right. "You want to meet Bentley?"

"Bentley?" she said, giggling. "Yay."

He stopped in front of a stall with a pretty bay mare who had a small white spot on her nose and a forelock so thick and long her eyes peeked out from behind it.

"It looks like she's wearing a wig, doesn't it?"

Jayden couldn't help but smile. She'd had the same thought over the past week. She'd never seen so much hair sprouting down a horse's face.

"What wig?"

"It's something people wear on their head." He moved closer. "You can pet her if you want."

And all Jayden could do was stand back and watch. It'd been so long since she'd watched a man hold her daughter like that. Lord knew Levi spent as little time as possible with her. Uncle Bob played with her, but he was too busy to spend a lot of time with her. Sure, she had lots of brothers, but they were all off living their lives, having their own children. Their time on the rodeo circuit meant their visits were few and far between. Carson was off building his new house, and when he wasn't doing that, he was focusing more and more on training rodeo horses and leaving the cattle operation to her other brother Maverick. And Flynn was always traveling with her dad showing horses. Shane was off traveling with his race-car-driving wife. Clearly, though, Paisley needed some man time. Her little girl soaked up the attention. Colby captured Paisley's hand, his bulging biceps making his brown T-shirt ride up his thick arms, and she caught a glimpse of a tattoo.

A tattoo.

She never would have figured he'd be the type. He

seemed…too straitlaced. The kind of man who would never mark his body with permanent ink.

Sunlight from the end of the barn aisle drew an outline around the two of them, her daughter's hair so light, his so dark. He guided Paisley's hand toward the mare, but as she was about to touch her, the horse sneezed.

They both jumped back.

"Euuuw," Paisley said, and Jayden couldn't help but laugh. "Bad horsey."

Colby glanced over at her, and they shared a smile, and it made Jayden's heart do something strange.

"How old is she?" he asked.

"Nearly four."

He nodded. "Why don't you use the phone again to see if you can find someone else to watch her?"

Was he sending her away?

"Okay." But she stood there for a moment longer. She couldn't help herself. Here was a man who seemed so chilly at times, and yet he held her daughter so tenderly and so carefully that she finally turned away out of self-preservation. Too many crazy thoughts had entered her head. She had to force her feet down the aisle, but she was back less than fifteen minutes later.

"I can't reach anybody." She ran a hand through her ponytail. "It's like there's a zombie apocalypse or something. Everyone's gone."

"What 'pocolypse?" Paisley's eyes were wide.

"Nothing, honey." She splayed her hands. "I don't know what to do."

"Nothing you can do but go home." He set Paisley down, catching her hand before she dashed off again, and then leading her toward Jayden. "I'll call the boss and let him know what's up."

"Please don't do that." She took Paisley, her tiny fingers sliding into her own in a way that always left her feeling protective. "I can stop on my way out." She swallowed. "But you're right. I should probably take her home. She'll only get in the way here. But I'll make it up to you, Colby, I swear. I'll work extra hours tomorrow. Or I can come back. I'm sure someone will return my calls. Eventually."

"Nah. Don't worry about it. We only have one guest. No big deal."

She had to reform her opinion of him right then. He wasn't the tough-nosed son of a gun she'd thought him. Behind his stern countenance was a man with a soft heart. It was like waking up in bed and realizing you were all twisted about and facing the wrong direction. She had to right the image in her head with the reality of the man who stood in front of her.

"I'll call you and let you know if I'll be back." She touched Paisley's soft blond hair. "Say goodbye to Colby."

"Bye-bye," said her daughter with a smile that would have melted the Grinch's heart. "He's nice," she said as they turned away. "I like him."

Jayden liked him, too. Liked him more and more, and that was a problem. A really *big* problem for a single mother who'd sworn to be sensible instead of headstrong. Getting involved with a coworker was exactly the kind of reckless behavior her dad had claimed she'd never grow out of, the reason he'd wanted her to move back home. He'd wanted to keep an eye on her, help her to "fly right." She'd never been so insulted in her life.

She could fly right all on her own.

* * *

Her car wouldn't start.

It took Colby a moment to identify the *click-click-click* he heard coming from the parking lot. The woman was having a hell of a day. When he exited the barn aisle, he saw her peering at him from behind the windshield, her eyes filled with disbelief and dismay.

"Battery," he mouthed. He lifted his fingers to his throat, giving her the universal sign to cut things off, then motioned her out of the vehicle. Paisley sat in the back seat, staring at him curiously.

"It's just not my day." She didn't bother to close the driver's-side door, just rested her arms on the roof of her silver Ford. "I think I should go home and go back to bed."

He'd like to join her there.

His cheeks reddened as if the words had been a physical blow. What the hell was wrong with him? He'd never allowed himself to even think about having a relationship with a woman. Not after everything he'd been through. Not after all the terrible things his ex had said, things that he'd known were rooted in truth. He'd moved away from Texas and settled in California and shoved Liz's astute assessment of his character out of his mind.

"Open the hood."

His words were brusque, and he kept his eyes averted, angry with himself for having untoward thoughts about his coworker. Damn old car. The engine was covered in a film of greasy grime, the scent of burned oil more pronounced once he ducked his head under the hood.

"How many miles you got on this thing?"

She didn't answer right away. "Over two hundred thousand."

Yipes. "Your battery cables are completely corroded."

"Can you fix them?"

She came around the side of the vehicle. A breeze brought her scent to him. Cherry blossom. That was what it reminded him of. "Or maybe clean them?"

"I can try."

But it didn't help. He tried jumping her vehicle next, and when that didn't help, he checked the solenoid.

"Bad starter," he pronounced.

He'd have to have been a real jerk to be immune to her crestfallen expression. "But I just drove it."

He shook his head. "Happens that way sometimes. They can short out."

"How do I fix it?"

"Buy a new one, and I'll put it in for you."

It was one of those moments when he instantly wanted to call the words back. What in the heck had he offered to do that for?

"You don't have to do that." She glanced at Paisley, who sat inside the vehicle, coloring. "I'm sure one of my brothers will know how to fix it."

Saved by the bell. And then he heard himself ask, "How are you going to get your car over to them?"

Her mouth dropped open slightly. "I guess I'll have to call a tow company."

"Don't do that. I'll drive you into town. I'm sure one of the local auto parts stores has a starter in stock. I can fix it right here."

What the *hell*?

He should be calling her a tow truck.

"Oh my goodness, if you could do that." She looked like she wanted to jump into his arms and shower his face with kisses, which might just be wishful thinking on his part, and that had him wondering if he'd lost his damn mind.

"It's no problem. We can always put the part on the ranch account, too. Mr. Stone won't mind. I'll ask him, but I'm sure he won't mind."

The flash of relief in her eyes told him. She clearly had to make her own way in the world. Fixing her car wasn't in her budget, and he couldn't seem to stop himself from helping her out.

"I can pay him back."

"Don't worry about it." He took a deep breath. In for a penny, in for a pound. "Why don't you and Paisley stay here while I go into town? I'll pop in at the boss's house on the way out, explain what's going on and that maybe he should have his chat with Bryan now."

He saw her take another deep breath. Saw her lashes sweep down and her mouth tremble, and he knew she fought back tears of gratitude, and on the heels of that thought, he knew life hadn't been easy on her. "I don't know how to thank you. If Mr. Stone says it's okay, please tell him thank you, too. Really. You guys have been great to me."

He could think of a few ways she could thank him. "Stay here. I'll go call the boss."

He couldn't get out of there fast enough.

Chapter 7

If she could have kissed him, she would have. Instead she watched him drive away, hoping that he was right and that Jax wouldn't mind him taking off to help her get her car started.

"Paisley, honey." She opened the car door, smiling when she caught a glimpse of what Paisley had been drawing. A brown stick horse with a fuzzy forelock that looked more like a giant asterisk. Bentley. "Let's go for a walk."

"Horsey?"

"Sure." She un-clicked the car seat, and as always happened, Paisley wiggled out of the thing like a puppy out of a collar. "After we're done."

At least she didn't run into the barn this time. That'd been so embarrassing. Instead Paisley took her hand and said, "Mama, pretty."

"Do you like this place, honey?"

"Yes."

It *was* pretty. Everything so new and clean. The scenery, with acres of pastures and forests of trees, was spectacular. Their veteran guests must find these surroundings soothing after all they'd been through. Before Levi had arrived and spoiled everything, she'd been coaxing a smile from their new guest, trying to get a feel for his personality, hoping to connect with him. He'd need physical therapy and counseling for his PTSD, all of which would be provided for him at the ranch, and since he was the first guest of the season, she'd been hoping to make a good impression, too. Thanks to Levi, she'd blown that within the first five minutes of meeting him.

"Where going, Mommy?"

Paisley's little legs had a hard time keeping up, so Jayden bent and pulled her into her arms. Her daughter's hands slipped around her neck automatically.

"We're going to talk to the owner of this place." Sure, Colby had said he'd do that, but she felt bad having him do her dirty work. Plus, she really wanted Jax to know how bad she felt firsthand.

"Who's that?" Although the words came out sounding like "Who's dat?"

"His name is Jaxton, and with any luck, he won't mind us doing some chores together." Hopefully Paisley didn't pick up on her anxiety. "You could help me sweep the aisle or something. Would you like that? We could even clean saddles together."

"Yes!"

If Jayden had asked her to pick up horse poop, Paisley would have been okay with that, too. She'd inherited the horse-lover gene for sure.

They walked across the parking lot in front of the cabins, their feet crunching on the gravel, Jayden wondering if Bryan peered out at them from the other side of the glass.

"Mommy. Look." Paisley's chubby little finger pointed. Jayden knew she'd caught sight of the Stone family home, which wasn't really a home, more like a mansion. It had come into view around the bend.

"Isn't it pretty?"

It looked like a resort, all angles and glass and thick beams and redwood planks. On such a beautiful day it sparkled like a geode beneath the late-morning sun. The house was built into the side of the hill, too, and overlooked a valley studded with oaks, a blacktop road intersecting the view, one as straight as a needle that pointed toward the front gate. She'd half hoped Colby would still be there, but his truck was nowhere in sight. There were no cars parked on the asphalt strip along the front of the home, either, making her wonder if anyone was home.

"Down."

Paisley was insistent, and Jayden knew why. She'd spotted the stairs that led to the front door. She loved stairs almost as much as horses, and these led to a porch that surrounded the home. She had to help Paisley navigate, but her daughter managed them with surprising ease. Jayden could hear voices inside.

"I said give it back."

It was a girl's voice, or maybe a teen.

"Not until I see what's on," replied someone else, a boy, by the sound of it.

"Darn it, T.J. Now. I'm right in the middle of watching something."

She rang the doorbell. A deep-throated *woof-woof*

broke the sudden silence. She and Paisley both jumped back. A second dog joined in the fray, and the second dog sounded scarier than the first, so much so she wondered if she shouldn't pick Paisley up before the door opened.

"Thor, *ruhig*," said a female. "You, too, Tramp. Quiet."

The dogs instantly hushed. The sluggish thud of what could only be teenage feet headed toward the door, followed by the *tap-tap-tap* of dog claws on a floor. A young lady with brown hair and pretty blue eyes opened the door a crack.

"Can I help you?" She stared at her, the space between her brows puckering, even more so when she spotted Paisley hiding behind her legs.

"Yeah, hi. I was hoping to talk to your dad."

The doorbell rang. Jayden glanced down at Paisley in surprise. The dogs went nuts again. The young girl quickly slammed the door, and Jayden heard her ordering the dogs to be quiet. Paisley. The little stinker. She'd pushed the button. Jayden scooped her up in her arms.

Only when the dogs were silent again did the door open one more time. "I'm Jayden Gillian," she told the teenager. "I work for your dad."

"Oh, yeah. Okay. Let me go get him." She stepped back, revealing a grand entry that would have done the White House proud with its marble floors and vaulted ceilings. A gorgeous German shepherd with a graying muzzle sat at the end of the hall. Tramp wasn't half as well behaved. He bounded forward.

"Tramp, no."

The dog skidded on the marble floor, and to his credit, he stopped.

"Da-ad!" the teen called.

"Will we be okay?" she asked, motioning toward the German shepherd.

"Oh, yeah. He's fine. Thor, *bleib*." She motioned with her hand. "That means 'stay' in German," she added. "He's an ex war dog."

"Who is it?" A boy with glasses peeked his head around a corner.

"Jayden. The new therapist Dad was talking about." She glanced down at Paisley. "And her daughter."

"You're the one whose car broke," said the boy, presumably T.J.

"I am."

"All right, you guys. T.J., give Sam back whatever it was you took from her." Jax came toward them from the back of the house. He smiled in her direction, still wearing the casual polo shirt and jeans from before. Tramp bolted toward him. "Kids, take the dogs with you."

The kids came forward, each grabbing a collar.

"I was just about to go down and get you."

"Jax, I'm so sorry about today. I had no idea my ex would show up."

"And who do we have here?" he asked.

Jayden followed the direction of his gaze. "This is Paisley." She clasped her daughter closer. Her three-year-old always seemed to ground her in ways Jayden would have never thought possible, and today was no exception. Holding her hand gave her confidence. "I hope it was okay to bring her by. I was thinking maybe the two of us can still do some chores. The saddles could use a good dusting off, and I could clean the empty stalls."

"Don't be silly." He motioned her inside. "Come on in and meet my wife."

"That's okay. Really. I don't want to intrude."

"Mommy," Paisley whispered, or tried to. She wasn't very good at regulating the volume of her voice. "This is a big house."

She almost laughed. Yes, it was big. With its grand staircase and a sunken living room to the left, it looked more like a hotel lobby than a home. But it was the smell that drew her attention. Garlic. And if she didn't miss her guess, bacon.

"You're not intruding." Her boss must have read her expression of pure delight. "We're just about ready to have brunch. As a matter of fact, I was about to go find you and ask if you wanted to eat with us."

"Yum," Paisley said when she caught a whiff of whatever was cooking. Her daughter seemed part blood-hound when it came to her favorite foods, and bacon was at the top of the list.

"That's my wife's gourmet BLT." He winked down at her daughter. "Tomatoes sautéed in garlic and basil. Maple-cured bacon. Spinach instead of lettuce. Equals heaven."

"I'm hungry!" Paisley said, her eyes so full of hope-ful anticipation that it made Jayden laugh.

"Then I guess we accept," Jayden said.

"Good." Jax motioned her forward. He led her through a wide entrance, living room left, hallway to the right. They passed a sweeping staircase and entered a gorgeous kitchen with a terra-cotta floor and a center island as big as a Ping-Pong table, one covered with off-white marble.

"This is my wife, Naomi," Jaxton said, pointing toward a double-wide stove where a woman stood cooking. "And my son Tanner in the corner there."

"Hey there," said his wife, turning toward her, and, wow, she was beautiful, made even more gorgeous by a set of pretty blue eyes that were alight with welcome. She had red hair that was pulled into a ponytail. She waved, metal tongs in her right hand. "I'd come give you a hug, but I need to turn my bacon."

"Baby!" Paisley said. She began to wiggle in Jayden's arms.

"Whoa there." She caught a glimpse of a little boy, probably no more than two, sitting on the kitchen floor playing with something behind a white baby fence. He played so intently with whatever it was on the ground that he didn't even look up when they entered.

"I wanna play!" Paisley said.

"Oh, no, honey. I don't think so."

"It's okay." Naomi half turned. Some women looked terrible with their hair off their face. Naomi Stone could have passed for a model with her heart-shaped face. "You can put her in there with him."

"Are you sure?"

"He plays with his cousins all the time," Jaxton said. "One of them is two years older and they do just fine. Go ahead."

She rounded the corner of the center island. The most adorable blue-eyed boy looked up at them as they approached.

"Hi, Tanner," she said softly. "This is Paisley."

Her daughter just about jumped out of her arms when she leaned over the plastic fence. She immediately toddled over to Tanner, pausing a moment to stare down at the little boy, who eyed her curiously, then bending to give him a hug.

Her softly spoken "Hi" melted Jayden's heart.

"That's the most adorable thing I've ever seen," her boss said from behind her.

"She's got a good heart."

"I can tell," Jax said. "Probably a lot like her mom."

"I heard about your car." Naomi turned away from the stove again, the stainless-steel hood above her whirring, the bacon she cooked sizzling and popping grease onto the brick backsplash. "Bummer." She put the tongs down, wiping her hands on the front of her apron before meeting her husband's gaze. "Did you check on Bryan? Did you invite him to lunch like I asked you to? Are you sure, I don't know, we shouldn't have him stay with us until the other vets arrive? You guys were such good friends."

"Relax," he said, going up to his wife and giving her a kiss on the cheek. "One, I never even left the house. Jayden was at the front door as I was about to leave. Two, I tried calling him, and he didn't answer. Three, I'm guessing by the tersely worded message he left me after I told him we needed to talk that he wants to be left alone, but I'll go ask just to be sure."

"Oh, well, shoo." She waved her husband out of the kitchen. "Tell him I said hello. I'll set up brunch on the back patio."

"You know you don't have to cook for our guests anymore. Patsy will be over in a little bit. She'll get Bryan squared away if he refuses to eat with us."

"Patsy can come eat with us, too."

"You're doing her job."

"She has enough to do, what with keeping this place

clean and helping me with the kids. Besides, I did her job long before she moved in, so it's no big deal." She waved at him again. "Go. It'll be done in a few minutes."

He just shook his head. "Be right back." He waved at her as he left.

"Sit." Naomi motioned toward the bar stools stashed beneath the center island. "I'm just about to pull the bacon off the stove. I'll toast some bread next and then we'll be ready to eat."

"Smells amazing."

"It's my kids' favorite," she said over her shoulder as she flipped over some more bacon. "We all sort of overslept this morning. My sister-in-law had a party last night. Do you know Lauren Connelly?"

"I've heard of her. She's the sheriff's wife, right?"

"That's her. She's a nurse over at Via Del Caballo General. Great gal. You'll love her."

"Her husband's super nice." She'd had to call him a time or two when things had gotten heated with Levi. She'd never forget his kindness.

"Anyway, Patsy is our housekeeper. She lives in the apartment right over there." She pointed to a door by where the kids played. "She cooks and cleans for our guests. And when we don't have guests, she helps me around here. I started an event planning business a couple years ago, so it gets a little crazy sometimes."

"You plan weddings?" Jayden couldn't remember where she'd heard that, maybe her aunt.

"Yup. We actually hold them here in the spring and fall. That's on top of the work we do with veterans. We've always got something going on around here, but I wouldn't change it for the world. We are so blessed."

She had a feeling she'd get along great with her boss's wife. She was older than her by a dozen or so years, but her smile was so warm and friendly, Jayden felt instantly at ease.

"If you want to do me a favor, could you get some plates out and put them on the patio table? I'm going to scramble some eggs just in case someone's in the mood for a traditional breakfast."

"Sure."

"Plates are right there."

She pointed to a cabinet by a sink in the middle of the far wall. Jayden kept an eye on the kids as she went about her task. Her boss's home was amazing. On her way past the house earlier she'd thought it was built into the side of the hill, but that wasn't the case at all. It was angled in such a way that only the one corner touched the rocky outcroppings. A terra-cotta patio ran along the back side of the house and framed a pool made to look like it'd sprouted from cracks in the earth. A table sat right outside the door, near an outdoor stove made from the same bricks that formed the backsplash inside the kitchen. And what a kitchen. Wooden beams intersected the ceiling above. Bowl-shaped light fixtures— three of them—hung in a row down the length of the center island. You could probably feed every cowboy within a fifty-mile radius out of the place.

"Be nice," she warned Paisley when she took a yellow brick from Tanner. Her daughter immediately gave the piece back.

"I hope you're hungry," Naomi said.

"Come to think of it, I didn't have breakfast this morning. I was too busy running around trying to find a backup babysitter for Paisley. My aunt usually watches her for me, but she came down with a cold at the last minute. But then my ex showed up, only to drop her off here an hour later. I swear, he had no intention of watching her all day in the first place."

Naomi made a moue of sympathy. "I take it he's not the best dad?"

"That would be putting it kindly."

Naomi nodded. "I was lucky with my first husband. He might have had other faults, but he was a great dad." Some of Jayden's curiosity must have shown on her face because Naomi added, "T.J. and Sam aren't Jax's kids. Well, they are in every way that matters." She smiled, but it was a grin tinged with sadness. "Their dad died in combat."

Jayden's breath caught for a second. "I'm so sorry."

"It's okay, but that's why Jax and I are so passionate about this place. We've both been affected by tragedies. Everyone who works here has been touched by war somehow, even Patsy. And now Bryan is here." She shook her head. "Jax loves that man like a brother. The two of them were in the same unit years ago. Jax left, but Bryan stayed in."

Everyone? Even Colby? She was dying to ask. Instead she said, "I heard Bryan almost died."

"He did, and now he's got some psychological issues. They're some of the same problems Jax had when I first met him. This place was such a balm to his soul back then. For Colby, too. I hope it has the same effect on Bryan."

There it was again. Colby.

"Was Colby a guest here?"

"No, no." Naomi took a bite of bacon, chewing and clearly enjoying the taste. "He came to us from Texas."

Why did she think there was more to the story than that?

"He's a really nice guy, but he keeps to himself. I don't even think he's dated anyone in all the time he's been here. Shame, though, don't you think? He's really cute."

She tried to appear as if she hadn't a clue what Naomi was talking about, but her boss's wife had sharp eyes. She started to smile, the grin spreading across her face, amusement lighting her eyes.

"Aha." She pointed at her, laughing. "I see you agree."

She couldn't hold Naomi's stare. Darn her for bringing it up. She'd been doing fine ignoring her coworker's good looks up until the moment he'd pulled her up against him, and now here she was, blushing like a teenager.

"I think, though, that what he really needs is a friend."

Was she trying to tell her something? There was something in the depths of her gaze, something both serious and sad.

"I'm not sure he likes me enough to want to be my friend."

Naomi shook her head. "He likes you. You should have heard him earlier. He was singing your praises in that cute Southern accent of his."

She ducked her head. He liked her? Not *that* way, of course, but he approved of the job she'd done. That meant more to her than… Well, it just meant a lot.

"So I guess what I'm trying to say is don't let him scare you off. He might seem standoffish and hypercritical, but inside, he respects how hard you're working."

She supposed she liked and respected him, too. And that was scary to admit. The last man she'd liked had led her down the garden path. But that wouldn't happen with Colby. He was…different. Look at how he was fixing her car. Not many people would offer to do that. That was something a friend would do. There was nothing wrong with returning that friendship.

Was there?

Chapter 8

"All fixed," Colby said, slamming the hood of Jayden's car. He wiped his hand on a rag, grease coating his fingers. "Go ahead and try to start it."

Jayden slipped into the driver's seat of her car, foot hanging out, door still open. She'd told him Paisley was up at the big house, Colby trying not to feel self-conscious as he stood in front of her vehicle in his blue coveralls. He'd been great at ignoring women for so long, but he couldn't ignore this one.

"Here goes," he heard her say.

It started right up.

Her grin was as bright as a spotlight. She all but jumped out of the car, hand raised in victory. "You did it. Thank you so much."

"Go ahead and turn it off."

Some of her joy faded, and he realized he'd sounded terse again. Damn it. He really didn't mean to rain on her parade. When she'd come back down from the house she'd had the strangest expression on her face. Made him wonder what she'd been talking about with his boss's wife. But then she'd gone inside, explaining that with Paisley up at the boss's house she could do her morning chores, and he couldn't help but admire her work ethic. She could have taken the easy way out and used Paisley as an excuse to sit around all morning. Not Jayden. She'd mucked stalls and ridden a couple of the horses by the time he'd finished with her car late in the afternoon.

"I guess I owe you dinner." She slipped out of the car, slammed the door and turned back to him with that damn funny look on her face again.

"Don't worry about it."

He grabbed a rag off the fender of her car, wiping his hands some more. He was a damn mess.

"No, really. I want to."

She'd stared up at him, her eyes imploring, hair still pulled back. He didn't want to go out with her, but not for the reason she thought. He liked her, probably too much.

"I don't expect anything in return, so don't worry about it." He stuffed his hands into the pockets of his coveralls. "I'm going to change. You may as well leave for the day. It's late."

She peered at him from beneath lashes that were thick and long. "Look, I really appreciate what you've done for me today."

But...? There was always a "but," wasn't there?

"But please don't brush it off like it's no big deal. It is a big deal to me." Determination propped her shoulders up in the next instant. "I'm going to bring you breakfast tomorrow." Her mouth lifted on one side. "It's my way of saying thank you for everything. Not just today, but for your patience with me while I learn the ropes around here and for saying nice things about me to Jax and Naomi."

She knew about that?

"I've never had a lot of guy friends, but I'd like to be yours." And then she said softly, so softly that the words were very nearly carried away on a sage-scented breeze, "I could really use a friend right now, and I have a feeling you could, too." She shook her head ruefully. "You saw what I'm dealing with. I feel like I'm raising a second child with the way Levi is. I just finished school. I'm working full-time at a new job. My aunt is great, but she's more like my mom. My brothers are always gone or too busy, plus I really don't like spending more time at my father's place than I have to, so that leaves you."

She smiled brightly up at him. She was like that kid at school, the one you met in the cafeteria, offering friendship when no one else would. And that was probably the weirdest thing he'd thought in a long, long time.

"Why don't you like to spend time with your dad?"

She shrugged, then looked down, and he realized it was hard for her to talk about. But she was willing to share, and the fact that she felt comfortable enough to talk to him about something that was clearly deeply painful, well, it warmed him up in a way he hadn't felt in a while.

"My dad and I…we're not exactly talking right now. I guess you could say we don't see eye to eye on some things, specifically the fact that I got divorced and how I'm raising my daughter. He thinks I should have stayed with Levi for Paisley's sake, and he doesn't think it's good for me to be away from her so much, which is kind of ironic considering he was never around when I was growing up, something I pointed out to him and… Oh, boy." She blew a hank of hair out of her face. "That didn't go over very well. He told me if I'm so determined to work myself into the ground and have my aunt raise my little girl, he wasn't going to help me by paying for school or rent or any of the other things he used to chip in for. The last two years have been hard—I'm not going to deny it. My aunt tries to help out, but I hate asking her because if my dad finds out it would cause World War III. So I've been on my own. And I'm doing okay. But it's still hard for me to pass my dad's place without feeling physically ill. Unfortunately, he lives across the road from my aunt." She smiled wryly. "My aunt Crystal watches Paisley for me, and thank goodness for that because I don't know what I would do without her."

If she'd said she was an orphan she couldn't have shocked him more. And the realization that she pretty much raised Paisley all on her own rocked him back on his heels. Literally.

"So I guess what I'm trying to say is you're an angel for repairing my car. Really. I couldn't have afforded to fix it on my own, and if it'd stayed broken that would have meant missing work and then what?" She lifted her chin. "I'd rather be dipped into a vat of hydrochloric acid than ask my dad for anything."

He understood. Probably more than she could ever know.

"So thank you, from the bottom of my heart." She came forward, reached for his hand. He didn't want to touch her, but he couldn't exactly ignore her.

He clasped her hand.

It was like being sopping wet and touching an electric wire. That was how much of a jolt it gave him. She jerked her hand away, and her eyes flickered, her shoulders tensed, all things a less astute man might have missed, but Colby saw it. He studied her closely, took the sum of her parts and judged them as a whole—the way she couldn't look him in the eye now. How she kept fussing with the gravel by dragging her toe through it. The way she played with her bottom lip as she stared at the ground.

She'd felt something when he'd touched her, too. Some kind of mutual crazy attraction.

Damn.

"You're nothing like I thought you were," he said softly, and he had *no* idea why he'd said the words.

He watched her throat work as she swallowed, Colby stunned by just how badly he wanted to expand on the comment, to try to reassure her how much he actually liked her. He couldn't, though. Wouldn't.

"And you're nothing like I thought you were, either." She took a step back. "I should go pick up Paisley. Naomi has watched her all day. I have to figure out who's going to take care of her tomorrow since I doubt my aunt will be feeling any better. I've already been a big enough pain. I won't let that happen again."

She turned and all but ran back to her car. Colby let her go. That was what he always did—what was best for everyone. Let them go. Too many scars. Too many nightmares. Too many bad memories. It was why he left Texas. He was better off alone. He didn't hurt people that way. Didn't close them out. Didn't drive them away…into someone else's arms.

She deserved someone better than him.

* * *

Dear God in heaven.

Jayden gunned the engine, her tires kicking up gravel, she backed up so fast. She took her foot off the gas at the same time her gaze hooked on Colby again. He hadn't moved. She turned the wheel, aiming for the road that led to her boss's house and away from him.

You're nothing like I thought you were.

She shook her head. And what was with the sadness she'd seen in his eyes? What was in his past that he didn't want to talk about? Why did she care?

She wished her mom were here.

For a moment she couldn't breathe. It'd been years, and yet it still happened from time to time, that terrible knot in her stomach, the ache that made her physically ill. Abigail Gillian had been her best friend in the world. She would have taken her side when it came to dealing with Dad. And she would have sat down and listened to her thoughts about Colby. Been the voice of reason. Because right now her mind was jumbled and she couldn't deny that when he'd touched her, she'd felt something.

She had to take a moment to gather the reins of control when she pulled to a stop in front of the Stone residence. Her fingers ached from clutching the steering wheel too hard, but the cool air felt good on her face when she got out of the car.

"Mommy!"

Paisley's cry of delight when Naomi brought her to the door was a balm to her soul. She needed to be sure she was always thinking with her head, not her heart, because that was exactly what her dad always said she did.

"I see he got your car fixed."

"He did." She opened her arms, taking Paisley from Naomi. "And I offered to take him to dinner as a way of thanking him, but he said no. So I'm going to bring him breakfast. Can I drop off some bagels or something in the morning, too? I can't thank you enough for helping me out today. I promise to work extra hours tomorrow to make up for the time I lost today."

"Don't worry about it." Naomi's face reflected the friendliness in her eyes. "You don't need to bring me anything. I'm just glad Colby was able to help you out."

And that was the moment she realized how lucky she was to have landed a job at Dark Horse Ranch. A job she would do everything in her power to keep, and that meant ignoring the spark of attraction she'd felt for Colby.

She drove home thinking about the best way to deal with Colby in the future. It helped that they'd be busy in the coming days. They had another guest arriving this week. They'd introduce Bryan to horses tomorrow, too. That would mean working with Colby at some point, but she'd be sure to keep things professional between them.

But the next morning saw her so nervous it made her physically ill. At least her uncle had agreed to watch Paisley while her aunt convalesced. She had the whole week covered, no thanks to Levi. She hadn't heard a word from her ex since he'd dumped Paisley on her the day before.

"You hungry?" she asked Colby, holding up a bag of breakfast burritos.

Colby stood in front of the barn holding the reins of two saddled horses, waiting.

"Bring them with." He motioned toward a saddlebag on the back of the horse he rode.

"We both riding this morning?"

It was chilly, a coastal fog having worked its way inland. She grabbed her black jacket with the sheepskin-lined hood out of the back of her car. He dressed in black, too, even his cowboy hat. She hoped that wasn't a reflection of his mood.

"We are. You can eat on the way if you get hungry. I don't have much of an appetite this morning."

Uh-oh. That boded ill for the day.

"Thanks again for fixing my car for me," she said, stuffing the bag in the saddlebag, all the while feeling so self-conscious she could barely look him in the eye.

"How's it running?" He glanced at her car, his eyes partially shielded by the brim of his hat.

"Perfect." She snuggled into her jacket. She should have gotten a latte or something at the coffee shop where she'd bought the breakfast burritos. "I take it I'm riding Bentley."

"You are." Not by word or deed did he reveal any recollection of their conversation yesterday. Back to the same old Colby.

"What time do we start working with Bryan?"

"Not until ten. We'll ride for a bit, come back and start the ground work with Bryan."

She told herself to look him straight in the eye as she took the reins from him, the leather still warm from his hands. She couldn't do it, though, had to shift her gaze to the ground or the horse or anywhere else but Colby. When she climbed aboard she headed straight for the arena.

Things might be back to normal for him, but not for her.

"No, not that way."

Her horse threw his head up, a reaction to the way she jerked on the reins. She instantly loosened them, chastising herself for being so distracted. "No?"

"Figured it's time I showed you the trails we use when we take veterans out to ride." He turned his horse away before she could frame a response, forcing her to kick her horse into a trot to catch up to him.

He went back to pretending as if she didn't exist, as he did the first couple of days they'd worked together. Last time they'd ridden together he'd given her tips on the horses she rode, or pointed out something she wasn't doing right. Now he was as quiet as a priest in a confessional box. Awkward. That was how things between them felt. Awkward and loaded with tension, at least on her part. She doubted he gave her any more thought than he gave the horsefly that buzzed around his head.

Fog poked hazy fingers over the tops of the hills. A light mist fell, the kind that seemed like it was snow, and clung to her hair and would've turned it into a frizzy mess if she hadn't pulled it back. She'd always loved early-morning rides when the smell of wet earth hung heavy in the air. Before her mother had died, they would frequently get up early and head out before morning chores. Her mom would have loved the weather this morning.

Colby stared at her.

She started, realizing that they'd stopped in front of a wooden gate, one that matched the white fencing that stretched off to the right and left.

"I'll get it," she said.

He rode up and unlatched it before she could do a thing, making her wonder what he'd been waiting for when he'd been sitting there staring at her. "Thanks."

They'd only followed the trail for a few hundred feet when he said, "You looked sad back there."

So he *wasn't* ignoring her.

She contemplated shrugging him off with an "It's nothing," but something, maybe her need for brutal honesty in the wake of her offer of friendship yesterday, had her saying, "I was thinking about my mom."

They rode on in silence for a moment, with only the sound of their horses' hooves scraping the ground. They headed toward some low-lying foothills, Jayden trying to focus on her surroundings instead of the man who rode next to her. Impossible to do.

"Sometimes," he said softly, "I find myself wanting to tell my mom something, but then I remember she's not around anymore, and even after all these years it still hurts."

That was so close to what had happened to her yesterday that her throat constricted and her hands clenched. She wondered if the pain of her past had stamped permanent lines on her face, ones that his own grief allowed him to recognize.

"I was thinking she would have loved this."

"Yeah." He looked around at the landscape and nodded. "My mom would have liked this, too."

"Hard to believe we get paid to ride out like this."

"One of the perks of the job."

She took a deep breath. "Naomi told me you came from Texas."

This was better. Conversation. The great equalizer.

"Once upon a time."

"Do you miss it?"

"The humidity, no, but I miss the dramatic weather. Real weather. Thunderstorms. Torrential downpours.

Snow. Not the tornadoes, though," he drawled. "Those I could do without. Some days I feel like this part of California is one big broken record. Same song playing over and over again."

She guided her horse around a puddle in the middle of the path. "I wouldn't know." She shot him a sheepish smile. "I've never been anywhere."

He glanced at her sideways. "I would think the daughter of a world champion cowboy would have been all over the place."

Her ponytail brushed her cheeks, she shook her head so violently. "We stayed at home with my mom. She was devoted to us. The best mom a girl could ask for."

Man. What was wrong with her today? She hadn't missed her mom so much since the early days of her loss.

"My mom was the same way."

"Then we were both lucky."

They had slowly climbed a slight rise, something Jayden hadn't noticed until she turned and looked back. The ranch sat below them, the arena still looking huge even though it was off in the distance. And from where they were, you could see the entire place, even the main house, with the soggy skies darkening the earth to an army drab all around.

"I don't want to mess up this job, Colby."

His horse had stopped even though she hadn't seen him pull back on the reins. "I don't expect you will."

His vote of confidence filled her with humility. She had a feeling he didn't hand out praise all that often.

"You've done great since you've started." It was hard to read what was in his eyes, but she thought she saw approval there. "I'll be honest—I expected you'd be a pain in my rear, but you're not."

A crow called to another crow in the distance. She turned her head to try to spot it, her thoughts swirling, suddenly nervous and on edge.

"Thank you."

He nodded, staring at her. She couldn't take it, had to look away.

"Race you to the top."

She didn't give him time to respond. Her horse needed no urging, her hooves kicking up clods of earth, Jayden's anxiety fading away as she held on for dear life, her cheeks catching wind-generated tears, Colby's horse gaining on her with each stride. And it felt good. Oh, how she had missed this, the utter freedom of galloping headlong on the back of a horse.

She beat him. Her horse didn't want to stop, and Jayden laughed when she managed to turn the mare in a circle, the frisky little thing crow-hopping a bit as she wound down.

"I won."

"You had a head start."

"Well, yeah. A girl's gotta do what a girl's gotta do."

"Cheater."

The wind had dried her mouth, but she had no problem saying, "You're just jealous because I'm a better rider."

"Oh, I don't think so."

But he was smiling. Lord have mercy on her soul. A real smile. His face was in profile, his chin more pronounced when viewed from the side. Smiling. It'd been a battle worth fighting for, because she hadn't liked what she'd seen in his eyes when they'd been talking about her mother.

Sadness.

It clung to him like it probably did her. She didn't know why she hadn't noticed it before. He'd hidden his sorrow behind a mask of indifference, she supposed. She saw it now in the way his smile slowly faded, the lines of his grief pressing down on his heart. Was that what she felt strumming between them? Some kind of subliminal understanding of heartache and loss?

"My mom and I used to have some of the best discussions in a spot just like this."

He seemed to gather his emotions in the same way he collected the reins. "Your father's place is right down the road from here, isn't it?"

"It is." She patted her horse, the mare shaking her head, still wound up. But Jayden settled her down, her gaze catching on the saddlebag.

"Hungry?" she asked.

"Sure."

So they sat there atop a hill overlooking the valley, each of them eating in silence, and she wondered if he was as damaged as some of the men and women who visited the ranch. Maybe she had it all wrong. Maybe it wasn't the loss of his mother. Maybe it was more than that.

"How long were you in the navy?"

"I wasn't in the navy." He smiled again, but it was a small one, the creases at the corners of his eyes getting a workout today. "I was in the army."

"Green Beret?"

"What makes you think that?"

She shrugged. "I don't know." And she really didn't.

"Something about the way you carry yourself. It was just a guess. I don't know anybody in the military."

"You guessed correctly. Hero of the modern world. Savior of the oppressed."

But the way he said the words told her something more. There had been sarcasm there. And self-reproach. Maybe even disgust.

"Did something happen to you when you were in the military?"

"We should head back." He wadded up the foil wrapper of his burrito and stuffed it in the saddlebag. She did the same thing. "We have more horses to exercise and chores to do." He didn't wait for her to answer.

"Colby." She caught up to him before she even knew what she was doing, pulling her horse up in front of him so that he was given no choice but to face her.

It was one of those moments where she felt as vulnerable as an actor on a stage, a spotlight beaming onto her and exposing her vulnerability. She hated how whatever she saw in his eyes affected her, tried to resist the urge to make it better. She'd thought she could "fix" Levi, too, and look where that had gotten her.

"If you ever need someone to talk to…"

He didn't say anything. She didn't expect him to. She should have left it at that, but of course she didn't.

"I know what it's like to keep things bottled up inside. It isn't good for you. When my mom died I didn't have anyone to talk to. There I was, surrounded by family, but I'd never felt more alone in my life. I swear, that's why I started dating Levi. If my mom had been alive, she'd have warned me away from him. But then I got pregnant, although if I'm honest with myself, I wasn't being all that careful. My dad was furious when

I told him. He's the reason I married Levi. I thought maybe marriage would fix things between me and my father, that maybe if Levi made an honest woman out of me, I wouldn't be such a disappointment to my dad. But then I ended up divorcing Levi. And then my dad had his heart attack and things really got bad between us because he thought I should have stayed with Levi despite what a jerk he was, so I said to heck with my dad. I refused to let him make me feel bad about my decisions and my choices in life. But I've been thinking lately maybe I should confront him, lay it all out on the table, tell him how much his cold shoulder has hurt me over the years, and how it's hurting his granddaughter. That's the worst part."

Once again she was opening up to him and she had no idea why. Maybe she really did need a friend.

"Paisley brings joy into my world, even though a part of me grieves for the fact that she'll never know her grandparents. Even when I caught Levi with another woman, I still had Paisley to hold on to."

She'd been staring at the tooling on her saddle, but she caught the way his head snapped in her direction out of the corner of her eye. "He cheated on you?"

She shook her head. "Mama always said to stay away from rough stock riders. They're a wild bunch. Turns out she was right."

She had his attention now, and she held his gaze because she wanted him to see that Levi might have hurt her, but he hadn't broken her. What she saw on Colby's face in return made her heart pound all the more. His jaw ticked, and his mouth had compressed into a thin line. She recognized the look: indignation. He was angry on her behalf. Her heart did a double take. He cared. He wouldn't have that kind of reaction if he didn't.

"It's okay. I'm over it, and him." She never wanted Levi back in her life again other than as a father to Paisley, and even that she really didn't want. "I guess my point to telling you all this is that I've been through a lot. I might be young, but I've had a lifetime of heartache, so if you ever need me, or if you ever want to, I don't know, share breakfast again, I think that'd be great. You know, just as friends," she quickly added, but then smiled. "If you ever need someone, I'm a good sounding board."

Why did her eyes suddenly well with tears? Weird how out of the blue it came, this urge to cry. She choked them off by kicking her horse forward.

She could feel him watching her the whole way back to the ranch.

Chapter 9

For the first time in his life, he didn't want to go to work. There was nothing he could do to avoid it, though, and so he left his own apartment above the arena when he heard Jayden arrive.

Right on time.

Crazy the emotions she raised within him. Like now. As he headed downstairs, the horses nickering a welcome the moment they heard his feet hit the first steps, he found himself clutching the rail for support. He felt the strangest urge to run back upstairs.

She didn't head directly inside, though, and he realized the reason why a moment later when he spotted her crossing the parking area and heading toward Bryan's cabin. She wasn't wasting any time. Right to work. He was relieved to do the same.

But he listened for her.

He couldn't seem to stop himself. He grabbed a broom to sweep. But discovered he didn't need to. The place was spotless thanks to Jayden, but even over the *shhh-shhh-shhh* of the bristles brushing the ground, he strained to hear.

"It's really pretty, isn't it?"

Just keep working. Don't look at her.

He turned.

She walked across the parking area, Bryan in his wheelchair to her left, her face a fascinating mix of frustrated impatience and concern. Bryan looked a mess. He clearly hadn't shaved since he'd arrived. His brown hair hadn't been combed, the gray in it more pronounced when unstyled. He jerked the wheels of his chair like he wanted to propel himself a half a million miles away.

"Anyway, and then Colby called me the next day and told me I had the job."

Bryan stared straight ahead, or maybe into the barn aisle. Colby couldn't tell. The veteran would be a handful. It was clear he wasn't thrilled to be at the ranch. Yesterday, he'd closed himself off in his cabin, refusing to work with them. Patsy said he'd refused to see his old friend, their boss, too, and that he'd barely eaten a thing when he'd arrived. No wonder he was so skinny.

"It's my dream job, really." Jayden kept talking, clearly determined not to let his bad mood affect her own. "You'll see. This place really grows on you."

When their gazes met, she silently telegraphed her frustration, shrugging a little. She seemed oblivious to the turmoil she'd created inside him thanks to her little speech up on the hill.

"You ready to learn a few things about horses?" he asked.

"No."

Bryan sounded like someone who'd been asked if he wanted an enema. It wasn't the first time they'd had a veteran who was less than thrilled to be at the ranch. Oftentimes, Hooves for Heroes was a last resort, friends and family begging their loved one to try hippotherapy, although their program had evolved over the years into more than just hippotherapy. They had a PT program and psychologists and a list of specialists who could be called in on a per-case basis. Sometimes just the hippotherapy worked; sometimes it didn't. Sometimes it took a combination of treatments. Bryan was a candidate for PT and hippotherapy and counseling, but it remained to be seen if he'd accept that help.

"Why don't you watch us show you how it's done from a distance, then," Jayden said.

Colby wouldn't be so nice. "Follow me."

Jayden stood back, Colby hating the way she made him hyperaware when he grabbed a halter off a hook, heading for Bentley's stall without looking to see if they followed.

"You'd be surprised how quickly horses can pick up on a person's mood," he heard Jayden say. "I swear, they can read minds."

Did Bryan snort? It had sure sounded like it. Colby slipped the halter on Bentley's head, leading the mare out of the stall. Jayden tried to push Bryan's chair toward the horse. He jerked away from her. She stepped back, clearly both hurt and disappointed. The man needed his butt kicked, but he understood the place he was in. Bitter. Disillusioned. Wanting to be left alone. He'd have to have a talk with her. Tell her not to take things personally. Some guys didn't want a woman to see them at their worst.

"This is Bentley." He stopped the horse by Bryan. "She's a ten-year-old quarter horse and she'll be yours to use for the duration of your stay."

Bentley knew the drill. She stretched her neck toward Bryan's wheelchair.

Bryan moved back a hair, but it wasn't far enough. The horse knew to look for treats, and so she had no problem sticking her nose in his lap. Bryan moved farther back.

"Go ahead and let her sniff you." Colby met Jayden's gaze. She looked like she wanted to smile. "She probably thinks you have a treat."

Bryan kept moving back. Bentley kept stepping forward. Colby finally tugged on the lead, and if Bryan's eyes had been a ray gun, Colby would have been a black spot on the ground.

"Just relax." He slid his hands up the rope lead. "Horses are like dogs. Hold out a hand."

"She can sniff me just fine while I'm sitting here."

"Suit yourself."

Bentley took another half step closer, the mare lifting her nose so that it was even with Bryan's hair. A fine dusting of shavings clung to the mare's long whiskers. Bryan leaned back in his chair, his hands clutching the wheels. The mare's nostrils flared as she breathed in and out, disturbing Bryan's hair, the man clearly not happy with the horse's proximity.

"She's not going to hurt you." Jayden's voice was soft. "She's memorizing your smell. Once it's imprinted on her mind she'll never forget it."

"I wish she would."

Jayden tipped her head down, but peered up at Colby with a look of impatience on her face complete with furrowed brow. When their gazes met, she seemed to ask him what to do.

"Go ahead and step back. I'm going to put her in the cross ties so you can get started grooming her."

The light in the barn aisle might still be dulled by clouds that hid the sun, but there was enough sunlight to see the irritation in Bryan's eyes. He didn't want anything to do with horses. Wow. Colby had no idea how Bryan's family had managed to get him to the ranch, but he would bet it had involved threats and maybe even blackmail.

"Just stay right there while I get Bentley squared away. Jayden, maybe you could explain the different types of brushes we use on a horse's coat."

"Sure."

He watched out of the corner of his eye as she went to the groom box hanging on the wall, pulling out some items to show Bryan.

"I can't hold those," Bryan said.

"Sure you can. You grab your wheelchair wheels."

"I can't lift my arms to brush. I can't even brush my own damn hair."

"Yes, I know, but that's why this is so good for you. It's a form of physical therapy."

Bryan sank into silence. Colby tried to think of a way to break the ice. He'd run into his type before, although they weren't usually this resistant. Most people had an avid curiosity about horses. Bryan seemed to be repulsed by the very notion of them.

"You don't need to go over any more, because I won't be doing any of it."

Colby's hands froze on the snap he'd been about to

attach to Bentley's halter. He turned back to the two in the barn aisle.

"But it'll be so good for you," she said.

"Yes, but I already know how to groom horses and ride." Bryan's chin had tipped up. "I grew up on a ranch. I don't need horse lessons. I don't need to learn how to groom one. I've done it all a million times before, but I can't anymore."

He spun away from Jayden, leaving her standing in the barn aisle, watching as he jerked the wheels of his chair as if he could thrust himself all the way to his cabin with one good push.

"Bryan," Jayden called.

"Don't bother." Colby finished clipping Bentley to the cross ties. "Let him stew for a bit. We'll try again later."

She shook her head, the sadness in her eyes hitting him square in the chest. She had a big heart, this single mother with the weight of the world on her shoulders. He admitted then that they had that in common, too. A deep desire to help people.

"So what do we do?"

He took a deep breath. "I'm not going to lie. This is the hardest part of the job. Some people don't want to be helped. He's angry. Bitter. At the point where he just wants to be left alone."

She tipped her head sideways, her ponytail falling over one shoulder. "Sounds like you speak from experience."

A denial hung off the edge of his lips, ready to fall into an abyss of half-truths and lies, but she'd been so honest about her own personal life, and so maybe it was time to do the same thing.

"Honorable discharge," he heard himself admit. "Wounded in combat." He tapped his right thigh. "Couldn't walk for the better part of six months. Had to move in with my dad and…"

He didn't finish the rest of the sentence, didn't need to. He could tell she'd put two and two together. But she didn't know it all. Didn't know about Liz. Didn't know what had happened between Liz and his dad. There were some things he couldn't tell her. They were too raw, too painful to admit.

"Anyway." He lifted his shoulders once. "I went and lived at a friend's ranch for a while. He got me riding again, and that was when I knew what I wanted to do for the rest of my life. I went back to school and the rest is history."

Not quite. There was so much more to the story than that. His time recovering. The pain of losing both his fiancée and his father at the same damn time. The overwhelming guilt he felt for surviving when so many of his team didn't.

A hand clutched his own. He hadn't even heard her approach. "I'm so sorry."

She ached for him. He could see it, and it made his heart ache with an emotion he'd never felt before. Her grip tightened. He gasped. Or maybe he didn't; all he knew was every nerve ending in his body jolted as if they'd come into contact with hot wire.

"Jayden."

She reached for his other hand, too. He closed his eyes. She was so warm, her skin so soft beneath his hardened hands, like a skein of angora, and he wanted to pull his hands out of her grasp, slide his fingers around to the back of her head and tug her toward him.

The sound of a vehicle on the driveway made them both take a step back. It was a car bringing them their next guest. They'd both lost track of the time. But they stood there, staring at each other, Colby's chest rising and falling more and more rapidly as he thought about all the crazy things he wanted to do to her, and he could see the same thoughts echoed in her eyes.

"I'll go greet our new guest." The words sounded as if they came from the end of a tunnel, even though they'd come out of his own mouth. "You can take care of Bentley, if you don't mind."

"I don't mind." Her words were low and husky, her blue eyes darkened by the thoughts inside her head.

"We'll talk later."

He took off before he could do something foolish, like kiss her right there in the barn aisle.

What had she been thinking?

She shouldn't have touched him. He'd just looked so sad. It'd drawn her to him in a way she never would have expected.

"This place is amazing," said Dylan Carlyle, their newest guest, a man who seemed far happier with his apartment above the arena than Bryan had been with his private cabin. "I can't believe how big it is."

Dylan had balance and strength issues thanks to a traffic accident. It'd been a surprise to learn Hooves for Heroes didn't just take veterans; it took first responders, too. Cops, firefighters, anyone who served the public. Dylan had tried conventional physical therapy but his progress had been so slow he'd sought out a different, more varied program.

"No expense has been spared." She pointed to the

other side of the arena. "There's an elevator in the back corner if you ever need it, and you might. Between our riding program and physical therapy, you'll be sore, but that's a good thing."

Dylan smiled up at her from his position a few steps below. Their female volunteers coming next week would swoon over the man. He almost looked Spanish with his dark complexion and dark eyes. He walked with a slight limp, too, and she could see the fine line of a scar running down his right cheek. Dashing. Like a swash-buckling pirate.

"You worked here long?"

His smile was as warm as coffee on a cold morning, and it was laced with a sugar she instantly recognized—male interest.

"Not long." They both paused at the bottom of the stairs. "I'm still learning the ropes."

"You done with your tour?" Colby asked, walking toward them, and Jayden's spirits sank. He'd stuffed his humanity back into its concrete bunker again, bolting the door closed so she couldn't see what he was think-ing. She supposed she should be grateful. They *should* go back to the way things were before she'd gone and held his hands.

"We were just finishing up." She injected the words with a peppy smile, or so she hoped. "He's all settled into his room. We were headed down to see the horses."

"I can take over from here. You can take your lunch." He motioned with his chin for Dylan to follow him.

Diss-missed.

She could practically hear the drill instructor in her head, but one of the good things about working at Dark Horse Ranch was its proximity to her family and, perhaps more important, Paisley. What she needed right now was to wrap her daughter in her arms, to inhale her unique scent and to remember that this job was too important to risk getting involved with Colby. She waved goodbye to the two men, but she could feel them watching her the whole way down the aisle.

Her car wouldn't start.

She sat there for a moment, disbelief causing her to clutch the wheel as if she could will the damn thing into submission. She tried again. Nothing.

Colby peeked his head out the barn. Dylan stood behind him.

She wanted to cry.

Nothing had gone right since the moment she'd started this job. Maybe God was trying to tell her something. She should quit before a house fell on her head.

"Open the hood," she heard Colby say.

She pulled on the lever to her left and the hood popped open, Colby and Dylan disappearing when they lifted the cover. The sky had cleared, the sun warming her when she stepped out of the car, a horse nickering in the distance.

"Sounds like a starter," she heard Dylan say.

"We just replaced it. Might be a bad alternator. They can ruin a good starter in no time."

"Or she got a bad part."

She crossed her arms in front of her, relieved the burning in her eyes didn't translate into tears. At least Colby could fix it. She hoped. Things could be worse. This could have happened while she'd been out running errands, stuck somewhere with Paisley and nobody to help.

"Never a dull moment with you."

She didn't take offense to Colby's words. She felt the same way.

"Can you fix it?"

"I'm sure I can, but at this point, I'm wondering if you should take it to a shop. They can run some tests I can't."

A shop? She couldn't afford that.

He must have read the look in her eyes. "I know someone in town. Former guest here. He'd do anything for one of our employees."

"I can't believe this."

Dylan moved to her side, placed a hand over her own, squeezing it gently, the gesture so reminiscent of what she'd done to Colby earlier that her gaze shot to his own before she jerked her hand away.

Colby straightened. Just for a moment she caught a glimpse of it, the squinty-eyed, pupils dilated, flat-mouthed look of disapproval.

"I'll call a tow truck and run you into town to talk to the guy."

"You don't have to do that. I can take care of it."

"I'm not giving you a choice."

Chapter 10

Sitting next to her was like having a powder keg in the truck while playing with matches. For the first time in his life he began to regret his self-imposed celibacy and its torturous side effects, especially when he sat next to a woman who made him rethink his decision of living as a bachelor for the rest of his life.

"I can't tell you how much I appreciate you doing this for me." She stared out the window at the hills in the distance and a sun that had lost its daily battle with the earth, sinking below the horizon with a splendid splash of color, as if it wanted to go out with a bang. "I can't believe how quickly your friend diagnosed my car."

His grip tightened on the steering wheel as he pretended to concentrate on the road ahead of him when he was doing anything but. She smelled like spring when the orchards were in bloom, and it was damn distracting.

"I should have pulled your alternator and had it professionally tested when I took your starter out. This is my fault, really. It never occurred to me that it could have a short and that's why it wasn't charging."

Restaurants and small local shops passed by in a blur as they headed back to her place, to an apartment complex he'd never heard of before, but appeared to be on a rough side of town.

"Yeah, but at least you bought a warranty. I won't have to buy a new starter all over again. Not that I've paid for the first one yet." Out of the corner of his eye, he saw her shake her head. "I can't believe all this. I'm so stressed I'm going to be fired."

"Relax." It was his turn to shake his head. "I told you Jax understands. These things happen."

"Yeah, but how am I going to get to work tomorrow?"

"I can pick you up." And even though he heard himself offer, he couldn't believe the words had come out of his mouth.

"You don't have to do that." She frowned. "Maybe my uncle has a vehicle I can borrow. My aunt Crystal's going to drop off Paisley later tonight. I'll ask her."

Coward. That was what he called himself, because it would really be no trouble. The ranch wasn't that far from downtown Via Del Caballo. Instead he said nothing as she directed him to her apartment, pulling to a stop in front of a two-story complex that'd seen better days.

"This is your place?"

He didn't mean the words as an insult. It just looked so different from what he'd expected he found himself asking the question, but when he glanced over at her he saw her chin lift.

"It's not much, I know, but at least it's mine. You should try going to school full-time and raising a kid all on your own because, goodness knows, Paisley's dad refuses to give me a dime for child support."

He stopped the flow of words coming from her mouth by touching her hand. He had to breathe deeply for a moment.

"I didn't mean it that way."

Didn't he, though? Wasn't that exactly what he'd thought as he pulled up in front of her place? Despite everything she'd told him, there'd still been a part of him that had wondered if she'd really struggled as badly as she made it seem. She had.

"You amaze me."

The words were so far from what she'd expected to hear, her eyes widened in surprise, or maybe they did so because he'd tugged on her hand, pulling her toward him, and he realized another truth in that moment: he could no more resist her than he could control the gravity of the moon.

"Colby." Her eyes had a question in them.

"I'd like to kiss you, Jayden."

"We shouldn't," she all but whispered.

"I know."

She looked away, her next words all but a whisper. "I think I want you to kiss me, too."

Still, he hesitated. He had many reasons to avoid kissing her, some of them so deeply hidden inside himself he only caught glimpses of them from time to time. But the obvious reasons, the ones he'd been listing in his head over and over again since she'd touched him, those he couldn't seem to recall as he stared into her eyes. That gaze drew him down, her inner light and goodness a whirlpool he could no longer fight, and so he let the current suck him down until, at last, her feathery soft lips rested against his own.

It zapped him like static charge on a windy day, the reaction so unexpected that his heart jolted in response, and he knew that he hadn't imagined the connection between them. She felt it, too. He heard it in the barely audible hum she emitted, a sound that turned into a moan. In every corner of his mind he told himself to stop. Instead he found himself spinning ever deeper into the vortex that was uniquely Jayden.

She released another soft little moan, and he admitted he liked hearing her make the sound. His hands moved to the line of her jaw, her skin warm beneath his palm, everything about her so small and delicate and so utterly feminine that it roused every protective instinct he had, and that was an emotion he'd never wanted to feel again. The realization blasted him with a cold dose of reality, one that felt like icy fingers on his heart.

He wasn't any good at keeping people safe.

"No," he groaned as he drew back. "We can't."

Rather, they shouldn't, but not for the reason she probably thought. He wasn't a war hero. Far from it. That was a secret he planned to hold close to his heart.

"You're right. We shouldn't." Her eyes had turned the most dazzling shade of blue. "But I can't seem to help wanting more."

He exhaled a breath that shook from the aftermath of his desire. "We need to forget this ever happened."

"But—"

"No." He didn't want to hear more. If she found out how close he was to throwing caution to the wind, it'd be all over for him. "I'll be the responsible one here."

Those spectacular eyes that showed every emotion dimmed for a moment. Her whole face flushed, from her cheeks to her chin to her forehead, and he knew she'd taken his comment wrong. He almost called the words back. Almost. Instead he started the truck, forced himself to stare straight ahead.

"I'll see you tomorrow."

The cabin popped from a change in air pressure when she pushed her door open. He carefully composed his face into a blank slate.

"I would never say anything to Jax, if that's what you think."

His hands clenched on the steering wheel, tighter and then tighter still as he fought the urge to leave the truck and pull her to him and kiss her like he'd never wanted to kiss a woman before, not even Liz.

"Yeah, well, I can't take that chance."

Her facial muscles ticked, as if he'd physically struck her. "I'd be taking a chance, too, you know. I've already pushed the limits of my employment lately. If we both got caught messing around—"

"We're not. So end of story."

Her blue eyes were so luminous and intense he knew he'd wounded her.

She slammed the door. He gunned it, slipping away from her like he'd left so many things in his life.

Jayden all but ran up to her apartment, and for the first time ever, she was grateful for Paisley's absence. Her eyes were burning as she slammed the front door and then leaned against it, but not from tears of shame. Oh, no. They were tears of anger and frustration and maybe even amusement at the absolute and utter ridiculousness of it all. What were the odds? How could it be that after all her hard work she'd finally landed her dream job only to work with someone she found attractive, but who didn't want her?

She scrubbed at her cheeks, took a deep breath. This had been the week from hell. If she didn't know better she would think God had other plans for her and her career. First Levi showing up. Then her car breaking down twice. And now *this*.

Someone knocked on her door. Jayden glanced at the clock and realized nearly a half hour had passed.

Aunt Crystal.

"There's Mommy." Crystal's smile was wide, her familiar blue eyes meeting her own. "Go on."

"Mommy!"

Paisley's cry was a balm to Jayden's heart, as were the arms that wrapped around her neck and held her tight when she bent to scoop her baby up. She squeezed Paisley back, probably too hard, because she started to squirm in her arms.

"Owie."

"I know, baby. I'm sorry." She'd needed that hug. It served as a reminder of all she'd been working toward and the future that was right there in front of her if she didn't go blowing it by getting involved with a man who made her forget herself in the same way Levi had done...and look where that had gotten her.

"Let's go to the family room and have a chat with Auntie, okay?"

Her daughter took her hand, toddling along until she saw her favorite toy on the ground, a plastic horse with a golden mane and tail that Grandpa had gotten her for

Christmas back before everything had gone south. She loved that thing.

"Horsey." She plopped down on the ground, sliding her tiny fingers through the silky mane. "Weeee," Paisley said with a giggle, which was the sound she made when she pretended to be a horse.

"She's getting bigger every day." Her aunt settled on the couch, a piece of furniture Jayden's brother Carson had made for her. It was the only nice piece she had.

"How are you feeling?" Jayden asked.

"Better. Much better."

"Good." She sucked in a deep breath. "Thank you so much for dropping her off."

Her aunt hugged her next. "Honey, you know I'd do anything for you and Pais." She drew back, clutching Jayden's shoulders and squeezing them a bit. "But I wish you'd let us do more. This rift between you and your father. It has to end."

"I know."

"Really?" Crystal asked. "Because I hate the way you sneak around the ranch. I hate the way you refuse to ask your dad for help. Speaking of that, if your vehicle breaks down again, you can borrow one of our trucks, but you should really ask your dad."

She shook her head. "I'm not going to call him and ask him for something. He'll just hold it over me somehow."

"But you will call sometime soon?" her aunt asked.

She took a deep breath, knowing that if she promised her aunt, it meant she'd really have to do it. But like she told Colby, maybe it was time.

"I will."

Crystal looked relieved. They both watched for a

moment as Paisley cantered her horse on the nutmeg-colored carpet. Jayden smoothed her hair back and re-alized her hands shook.

"It seems like just yesterday she was crawling," Crystal said.

Her aunt had a way of taking the stress out of a room. She'd always been that way. When Jayden's mom had died, Crystal had been the only thing to keep her sane. Her dad and her brothers had dealt with grief the way a lot of men did, occupying their time with other concerns and hiding their sorrow behind stoic eyes. Jayden had tried to do the same, but her grief had driven her right into Levi's arms. She'd sworn off men ever since… until now.

Her cheeks heated as she recalled Colby's kiss. Huge mistake, she knew that, but her toes curled when she recalled how it felt to be held by him.

"Okay, spill." Her aunt didn't wear reading glasses, but she still peered up at her as if she did, chin down, eyes unwavering, her long gray hair tucked behind her ears. "There's something else going on with you, I can tell."

Damn her red cheeks. They betrayed her as surely as a lie detector.

She thought about denying it. She had every reason to do exactly that. She didn't need Crystal to worry about her making another mistake in her life. But in the end, her need to confess outweighed her concerns.

"I think I have a crush on my coworker."

Crystal's face slipped into a mask of horror. "With Jax?"

Jayden gasped. "No." She looked heavenward, wondering how her aunt would even think that. "With Colby Kotch."

She released a sigh, because now that she'd said the words out loud, she could no longer deny it to herself. Something about the man made her think things no sane mother of a three-year-old should be thinking, especially when she'd worked so hard to gain control of her life.

"And you work with him?"

Jayden nodded. "He's a therapist at Dark Horse Ranch, but he wears a bunch of hats sometimes. I'm supposed to be helping him out—well, I *do* help him out, and so we've been working together pretty closely. We've been a little shorthanded lately, but the ranch manager will be back from vacation tonight, so things will settle down, but I'll still be working with him."

"And you like him."

The words were said as a statement, Aunt Crystal's stare as intensely scrutinizing as someone in law enforcement. Jayden saw a hint of dismay in that gaze, probably not surprising given how anti-dating Jayden had been since the whole Levi thing had blown up in her face.

"He's a good man." Jayden knew she sounded defensive, but she couldn't help herself. "You can tell a lot about a man by the way he works with horses."

"Who's the family?"

"You wouldn't know them. He's from Texas. Talks with a Southern accent and everything."

Crystal had a curious expression on her face. Then she grinned. "Where's your laptop?"

"Aunt Crystal, no. No snooping. He's just a nice guy

that I work with. No need to stalk him on the internet or anything."

"Why not? You never know what you might unearth. What if he's running from the law or something?"

Crystal got up, scanning the room, spotting Jayden's computer sitting atop the kitchen table. She headed right for it and lifted the screen and tapped the return key before Jayden could stop her.

"You should really have a password."

Jayden wanted to slam the lid closed. "And you should really keep your hands off other people's devices. I mean it, Aunt Crystal. You don't need to Google him. It's okay."

Paisley looked up from playing with her horse, her attention caught by the raised voices. "Your great-aunt Crystal has lost her mind," she told her daughter.

But Crystal ignored her. She pulled a chair out, its legs clawing at the kitchen floor, screeching in protest. She plopped down without giving her a second glance. Light from outside the kitchen window gilded Crystal's long gray hair. She'd had that color forever, a kind of blondish gray. Most people her age would have dyed it, but Crystal always claimed she loved her silver locks. It made people think she was smarter than she was, or so she was fond of saying.

"Let's see." A tongue peeked out between Crystal's teeth. "How do you spell *Kotch*?"

"I'm not going to tell you." She went and scooped up Paisley, soothed by the scent of her hair. Some days holding her daughter was the only thing that kept her sane.

"Down," she said, wiggling.

Jayden sighed. The older Paisley got, the more she resisted being cuddled. Worst part of her getting older.

Crystal tapped her fingers on the counter. "Hmm. I'll try *K-O-C-H*. And I'll put the words *Texas* and *oil*."

It wouldn't pull up, not when she'd spelled it wrong, but then Crystal's eyes lit up and Jayden knew she'd been wrong.

"The first thing that comes up with his name is Kotch Petroleum. *K-O-T-C-H.* Houston, Texas. Probably not the same family, but you never know." She focused on the laptop again, tapped a few more keys. "Let's see why his name is mentioned."

Jayden sank into her own kitchen chair, covering her face with her hands. "I can't believe you."

"Wait a second, Jayden. Is this him?"

She swung the laptop around. Jayden's gaze zeroed in on a picture, and at first she didn't recognize the smiling face that belonged to Colby. He stood with his mom and dad. He was young, probably in his teens. Some sort of society event, judging by the fancy dress Mrs. Kotch wore, a stunning woman with Colby's dark hair and blue eyes. Colby's parents must have gotten married later in life. They looked to be in their late forties in the picture. But it was from his dad that Colby got his handsome face, and she realized she'd caught a glimpse of what Colby would look like in a dozen years or so.

Pictured left to right: Heir to Kotch Industries International, Darren Kotch, his wife, Anna, and son Colby.

Heir to Kotch Industries.

"That is him," she said in disbelief. He was heir to an oil empire? That didn't make sense. What was he doing working in California, then?

"See." Crystal swung the laptop around again. "That's

why you Google. You never know what you might unearth."

She'd never seen her aunt like this before. She seemed morbidly fascinated with Colby and his family. Jayden gave up. Her aunt tapped a few more keys. "Looks like his mom died about fifteen years ago, probably not long after that picture was taken. Oh, look. The dad has a Wiki."

She wanted to plug her ears. Or maybe get up and go play with Paisley. She could build a tent out of blankets and hide in there with Paisley for the rest of her life.

"Looks like Dad remarried after Colby's mom died."

"Oh?" she asked despite herself.

"She was much younger. Pretty." Crystal pursed her lips. "They're divorced now. Wow. That didn't last long. Two years."

She felt like she was riffling through Colby's personal belongings. "That's enough, Aunt Crystal. Really."

"He's an only child." Crystal's brows lifted. "And if the information on his dad's page is correct, Colby is worth billions."

And you would never know. She'd never met a more humble man dedicated to helping others. But that wasn't the point. The point was, he was her kryptonite, a man who made her forget herself in a way that she knew could lead to trouble.

"He's never mentioned having money."

"The good ones don't."

"Not that any of it matters. He could be the Prince of Wales and I wouldn't care. We're coworkers. And I like him, but it can't go any further than that," she quickly added. "We all know what happened the last time I got involved with a man. I'm not going to make another stupid mistake, and believe me, this would be one."

But he'd kissed her.

She couldn't ignore that one incontestable fact. And when he had, he'd become a red-blooded male, one that made her toes curl and her heart pound and her breath rush out of her like she'd jumped off a cliff. Neither of them had been thinking about their jobs or the future or where their attraction to each other might lead.

"There's that funny look on your face again," Crystal said.

"That's my look of hunger. Time to make dinner. You want to stay and eat?"

"Are you kidding? I have to go home and cook for your uncle Bob."

She hoped that was the end of the Colby Kotch discussion, but she should have known better.

"You really have a thing for him, don't you?"

Jayden tipped her chin. "I do, but I don't like him enough to want to risk my job. If things went south, I'd have to quit. I'm not willing to go down that road. He isn't, either—trust me on that. We're just friends. And that's how it will stay, because I'm not a stupid teenager anymore. I'm a grown-up with a daughter to raise. That's what I have to focus on."

No matter how much she wished things were different.

Chapter 11

Aunt Crystal drove her into work the next morning.

"Is that him?" she asked.

It was, indeed, him, the man riding around the arena hell-for-leather, as if he sought to outrun his troubles from the back of a horse. The dark brown chinks he wore—short chaps that reached barely below his knees—glistened, the fringe matching the bounce of the horse's stride, the morning air so chilly the horse's breath left behind puffs of steam. Jayden would bet she was one of the "troubles" he tried to outrun.

"That's him." She glanced back at Paisley. Her daughter had fallen asleep on the way over. Oh, to be that young and carefree. What she wouldn't give to sleep the whole night through. "Just pull up by the entrance there."

Her aunt directed her SUV in the direction Jayden

indicated, but she didn't let the truck idle. Oh, no. She put the SUV in Park.

"You don't need to park. I can hop out."

"I want to meet him."

"Aunt Crystal, no."

"Why not? Paisley's asleep in the back. I can slip out for a couple minutes and shake the man's hand."

"He's working." She picked up her purse, clutching it to her like a Viking shield. "I need to get to work, too. We don't have time for social calls."

"Sure you do. You said yourself someone came back from vacation yesterday. It'll be fine." Crystal slipped out before Jayden could say another word, softly closing the door so Paisley wouldn't wake up. She headed for the covered arena where Colby rode a dappled gray. Jayden saw him glance over at them, doing a double take, no doubt wondering who the lady was in the Navajo print shawl, knee-high cowboy boots and jeans tucked into the tops. For a moment Jayden thought about heading for the horse stalls. Maybe she could hide inside one and stay out of sight for the rest of the day. Her aunt could handle this first meeting all on her own. What stopped her was the way Crystal waved Colby over, like some kind of pool boy she wanted to do her bidding.

Oh, dear goodness.

"You must be Colby," she heard her aunt say.

Colby pulled his horse up next to a wooden gate. Belle, the horse he rode, sneezed her approval of the unexpected break.

"And you must be Aunt Crystal."

Score one for Colby for remembering her aunt's name. She couldn't even remember when she'd told him what it was. Maybe last night? Everything before their kiss had become a blur.

"I just wanted say thank you so much for taking care of my niece."

"No problem." He patted his horse, resting the reins on the mare's neck. "Least I could do."

Her aunt glanced back at her, and Jayden didn't trust the look on her face. It reminded her of a politician just before they slammed their opponent in a debate.

"Maybe you'll let us make it up to you." Jayden caught a whiff of what was coming next, her aunt's machinations as foul as the manure pile out back. "We have a family dinner every weekend. You should come over. I'll introduce you to my husband and sons, and Jayden's brothers. We can get a little loud and raucous at times, but it's fun."

No, Aunt Crystal. No, no, no.

She didn't want to risk running into her dad. Unless this was her aunt's way of forcing her hand and ensuring Jayden spoke with him.

Colby didn't seem enthusiastic about the idea, either. He glanced in her direction, but only for a split second, and in the moment she saw dismay hidden in the lines of his face. He didn't want to spend any more time with her than absolutely necessary, too. Well, that made two of them.

"That's mighty nice of you, Crystal, but I'm going to have to decline."

His Texas accent seemed more pronounced all of a sudden. A waxing of the Southern charm to take the sting out of his refusal?

"Well, now, Mr. Kotch, I wouldn't feel right if I let it go that easy. How about next weekend?"

"It's Colby." He rested his arm across his horn. "And I'm gonna have to check my calendar. Okay if I get back to you?"

Aunt Crystal knew when she'd been outmaneuvered, and she seemed none too pleased, too.

"Well, sure." Crystal smiled up at him sweetly. "You can tell Jayden what weekend works best for you. I'll even pop in and invite your boss, too. Make it a whole neighbor getting to know neighbor thing. You know what? I'll just tell Jax what day."

And that was how you turned the tables on someone. Jayden stared at her aunt in mute wonder. Never underestimate a former rodeo queen—they knew how to think on their feet.

"Well..."

Her aunt turned. "Gotta go now. Paisley's in the car. We'll see you soon, Colby. Nice to meet you."

She winked as she passed by. Jayden hooked her arm.

"What if I don't speak to Dad before then?"

"You don't have to speak to him before then. You can talk to him at dinner."

Jayden started to shake her head.

"No," Crystal said, sounding as stern as when Jayden was a kid and got caught trying to jump her horse over a water trough—without a saddle. "It's time you ended this feud, Jayden. I want my family back together again, and this weekend is the perfect time to do it. But if you'd rather have a private conversation, so be it. Every time you drive by your dad's place you have the perfect opportunity to stop in. So you're just as much to blame for this rift as he is."

"But—"

"No buts. Talk to him, Jayden."

Her aunt turned away before she could say another word.

Easier said than done, Jayden thought later that week as she drove away from her aunt's house after picking up Paisley. She felt ready to hyperventilate. Down below, in a small valley, vineyards stretched to the left and right. The view should have calmed her with its familiarity. It didn't. Her aunt lived on one hill, her dad the other, and she had to pass the driveway to his place every day. Today was the first time on her way back from her aunt's house that she slowed down, making a left and heading toward the single-story Spanish-style home perched atop a hill.

"Here we go," she told her daughter.

"Where go?" Paisley asked, blue eyes nearly the exact same color as Levi's peering back at her.

"We're going to see Grandpa."

"Grandpa?"

"If he's home," she muttered under her breath. She'd thought about calling, had decided not to give him a heads-up. It'd be just like the stubborn man to not answer, and then if she left him a message, he probably would make a point not to be at home. She decided to wing it. His big truck was in the driveway, so she knew he was around.

"Come on, sweetheart," she said after slipping out of the truck, opening up the back door of the truck.

"What are you doing here?"

Oh, dear. She turned toward her dad, wincing at the scowl on his face.

"Hey, Dad." She swallowed. "I thought I'd bring Paisley by to see you."

"What do you want?"

She tipped her chin up. "Nothing. I graduated from college. I have a job. I'm working over at Dark Horse Ranch, doing physical therapy like I told you I wanted to do."

"Then why are you driving Uncle Bob's truck?"

Damn the man. He wasn't going to make this easy on her, was he? She turned back to Paisley. "Ready to meet Grandpa?"

"Leave the kid in the car."

The kid.

For the first time her own temper flared. She turned back to her daughter. "Hold on for a second, honey." She gently closed the door. She would not subject her daughter to her dad's foul temper. She turned back to her dad. "Listen, Dad," she said. "I stopped by tonight in the hopes that maybe we could bury the hatchet. I'm tired of sneaking around out here like I'm some kind of third-rate citizen. I'm sad that my daughter, whose name, I will remind you, is Paisley, hasn't gotten to know her grandfather. But most of all, I'm sick and tired of you thinking I'm ten years old and can't manage my life when all I've done over the past two years is work my ass off to make something of my life."

"I see you still have your foul mouth."

And suddenly the fight drained out of her. She took a deep breath, imploring her father with her eyes to meet her halfway. "Daddy, please."

He threw his shoulders back, and she knew she wouldn't get anywhere with him. Not tonight. Thank goodness she'd kept Paisley in the truck.

"What have I done that was so wrong?" she asked him. "Why do you keep punishing me for my mistakes? I know I'm a single mom. I know I don't have a husband. And I know you're disappointed in me because I left Levi and got a divorce, but, Dad, people get divorced all the time. Stop punishing me for it."

"I wasn't punishing you," he said softly. "I was trying to get you to grow up. Levi was a good man. The son of a family friend. You should have worked it out."

That did it. The man had no clue what he was talking about, and she refused to explain it to him. On second thought...

"You think Levi's a good man? Really?" She took a step toward her father. "You should ask him where he was week before last. You should ask him how much he's paid me in child support. You should ask him how often he watches Paisley." She glanced at the car. Paisley was staring at her with wide eyes, and she realized she could hear every word.

She lowered her voice. "I was hoping maybe you could be a father figure for Paisley since her own father is MIA, but I see I was wrong. Goodbye, Dad."

She all but ran for the driver's side, flinging open the door and ignoring Paisley's "What wrong?"

Damn the man.

She backed the truck out. Her dad hadn't moved.

"Nothing, baby," she told the little girl in the rear seat.

"Mommy?"

Paisley was what was most important in her life. Not what her father thought of her. Not her ex-husband, and certainly not the man who'd kissed her the other day.

But she still cried the whole way home.

* * *

He wasn't invited to Gillian Ranch. He was summoned. Jax sent him a text Thursday evening.

Dinner at Gillian Ranch this Sunday. See you there.

He read it and reread it, trying to figure out a way to wiggle out of it without seeming ungracious or rude. He came up blank, but that didn't stop him from trying.

"I'm not sure I can make it," he hedged when he sat down with Jax for their weekly meeting that Friday. It'd been a stressful week welcoming new clients, sorting out volunteers, working on schedules…avoiding Jayden.

Jax didn't say anything, and Colby grew more and more uncomfortable under his stare. One thing about his boss, he could spot a dishonest person from a mile away.

"I'll be disappointed if you don't go, Colby." Jax leaned back in his chair. They sat in his second-story office, a wall of windows to his right that perfectly illuminated Jax's intense blue eyes. "I was hoping to introduce you to the Gillian family. Jayden mentioned her family has some retired show horses that might work for our program."

He clenched the arms of the chair he sat in, the damn thing always uncomfortable, although maybe he was just feeling the effects of Jax's scrutiny.

"Jayden could probably tell us what they're like," he offered.

"Jayden hasn't worked with our program long enough to make an informed judgment."

In other words, he should go. "I'll see what I can do."

Jax smiled. "Good."

He told himself it was no big deal. He could avoid

Jayden at her family home just as easily as he had at the ranch.

So he set off that Sunday evening dressed in his best white button-down and freshly starched jeans, topping them off with a tan cowboy hat. Jax had suggested they take separate vehicles since his was packed with kids. That suited Colby just fine. It meant he could take off whenever he wanted, and the sooner that would be, the better.

As he pulled into Gillian Ranch, though, he couldn't help but be impressed. He'd been to some pretty incredible estates over the years, and Gillian Ranch would fit right in with the best of them. He drove at least half a mile, passing between rock walls on either side of the driveway, before hitting the main homestead. Nestled in a small valley, the ranch played host to a vineyard of several hundred acres, and a barn was on his right that at first he thought was a house, it looked so much like a Spanish villa. Only as he crawled by it did he realize it was a stable, one shaded by tall oaks, pastures out behind it, an arena out in front. Crystal's home sat up on a small hill to the left, within walking distance of the stables, but he passed another driveway to his right and he wondered if that was Jayden's dad's place and if he'd see him tonight. He had a feeling he wouldn't. Something about the way Jayden had been behaving all week. Tense and upset. Of course, that could be because of their own stupid actions.

He stopped when he got to the top. The place was packed with trucks and vehicles parked at odd angles in the front, forcing him to wedge his truck between two cars. He could hear voices coming from inside the single-story stucco home, and so he headed toward a heavy wooden door set beneath a porch held up by arches.

"Welcome," Jayden's aunt said, smiling. "Come in. Everyone's out back. I'll introduce you."

She let him pass, Colby's attention caught by the wall of back numbers to his right, his footsteps slowing.

"They're from the National Finals Rodeo," she said. "There are buckles and saddles all over the place if you're curious. More down at the house where Jayden grew up, but her dad's not coming tonight, so you won't get to see those."

And the way she said the words, Colby could tell she wasn't pleased.

"It's amazing," he said. Wow. He'd known Jayden's family all competed, but he had no idea of the scope of it all until that moment.

"Feel free to linger," Crystal said.

"No, that's okay."

She led him outside, through double doors with glass panes in them, and out onto a covered veranda with a trellis that held a grapevine of some sort. The longest table he'd ever seen sat beneath, and it was packed with people.

"Everyone, this is Colby Kotch, and that's Kotch with a *t*." He saw Jayden's aunt wink, followed the direction of her gaze and spotted Jayden, her dark hair hard to miss.

"Colby, I'd introduce you to everyone, but you'd never remember everyone's name. So this is the family. That's my husband, Bob, at the end there. You know your boss's family sitting by him. This—" she patted the shoulders of a man near her "—is Jayden's brother Flynn. He's in charge of the horse operation, and I understand he has some horses he thinks might work for your program."

"Nice to meet you," Colby said, holding out his hand.

"You, too," Flynn said, taking his hand. "Heard a lot about you."

He doubted anything from Jayden, who, by the way, ignored him. She was talking to Paisley, who sat in a booster chair next to her, the adorable little girl catching his eye. Her whole face erupted into a smile as big as the moon.

"Mommy. Look."

Mommy clearly didn't want to look. "I see him," he heard her say over a chorus of hellos. "No, no. Don't get up. Finish your snack."

"Go see Cold-bee."

"Paisley. Sit down and eat."

A man with dark hair and sideburns leaned in next to her. "You want to get big like your cousin Bella, don't you?"

Paisley nodded, looking at a dark-haired girl about nine or ten years old across the table from her.

"Then you better eat," said the man.

"I told Jayden to take you down to the stables," Crystal said.

Colby pulled his gaze away from the rest of the family, wondering who they all were.

"Might want to do that before the sun goes down," said Flynn. "She knows the horses I have in mind."

"Yes, go now," Crystal said. "I'll watch Paisley while you two go take a look."

He glanced at Jayden just in time to see Jayden's shoulders tense. "But she's eating."

"Jayden," her aunt said. "Colby came all the way

over here to look at those horses. Go on now. The adults aren't eating for a while yet, so you have time."

Jayden just shook her head, her long hair loose so it flipped over one shoulder. In her eyes he saw frustration. He didn't blame her. He felt the same way.

"Pais," she said to her daughter, "Auntie Crystal is going to watch you."

"Jax," Colby called to his boss. "You want to go, too?"

His boss smiled, shook his head. "That's your deal, Colby. I still don't know enough about horses to make an informed decision. You two go." He waved him off with a hand until his attention was claimed by his wife, the pretty redhead saying something to him sotto voce, something that made him laugh.

Jayden looked at him. He stared right back. She shrugged.

Damn.

Chapter 12

They didn't say a word to each other as they walked through the house and then headed down the drive.

"I take it you still haven't patched things up with your dad?"

She felt her cheeks turn as red as the sunset behind him, because just the mention of her dad filled her with a combination of anger and dismay. She hated that they'd have to walk by his place on their way to the stable.

"I heard your aunt's ultimatum the other day," he said.

She released a breath she hadn't even known she'd been holding, some of the tension leaving her shoulders. It was good to talk to him, good to have her friend back.

"I tried speaking to him earlier this week," she admitted. "Didn't go very well."

They lapsed into silence again, Jayden tensing the

farther down the drive they walked. Her father's house
came into view.

"It was brave of you to try to work it out."

She glanced over at him. There was approval in his
eyes, but also sadness, and it made her wonder what
had happened with his own father to cause such a rift.

"It's been years since I've spoken to my dad, too."

They'd made it to her dad's driveway, and the relief
she felt upon realizing his truck was gone was instantaneous. He'd known about the family get-together, of
course, had purposely avoided attending...thanks to her.

"Did you disappoint your dad, too?"

She said the words half-flippantly, surprised when
he didn't immediately answer. When she looked up at
him, he seemed deep in thought.

"Actually, I left because he stole my fiancée."

She stopped in the middle of the driveway, thinking
he was joking. The seriousness in his eyes convinced
her otherwise.

"He stole her how?"

He started walking, and she followed along. "I brought
her home with me when I was discharged from the army.
We were planning on getting married, but then things
started to change. I didn't realize what was going on until
I caught the two of them together."

She stopped again. He kept walking a few more steps,
but then turned back to face her.

"Colby, that's terrible."

He shrugged. "It happens."

She shook her head. "Not in a normal family, it doesn't."

"Who said I was normal?"

He started heading back down the hill. They were almost to the bottom now, the vineyards directly ahead, a

part of Jayden keeping an eye out for her dad, but he'd clearly left the ranch.

"When was the last time you went home?" she asked.

His chest rose and fell, he took such a deep breath. "The last time I saw my dad was the day he told me he was marrying Liz."

Liz. So that was her name. The woman who'd done so much to damage Colby's heart, because it was clear she had. They were alike, in a way, each of them wounded by a family member, each of them trying to make their own way in the world.

"I'm so sorry."

He shrugged. "I'm over it now."

Was he? Was he really? Somehow she doubted it.

"So, tell me about the horses you have in mind for our program."

Change of subject. She didn't blame him. It was hard for her to talk about her dad, too.

"There's two," she said, taking her own deep breath. "One of them is my old show horse."

Out of the corner of her eye she saw him nod. "What kind of show horse? You mentioned you rode cutting horses and jumping horses."

He remembered. Why did that make her flush?

"She's a cutting horse. Her name is Scarlett Kisses. Little sorrel mare who never took a wrong step in her life. She's older, but still in great shape. We tried to breed her, but we could never get her in foal. Dad would give her a home for life, but I think he'd rather see her put to good use rather than living in a pasture 24/7."

They'd reached the flat portion of the driveway, the stables to their left. When the sound of a rooster crowing reached them, Jayden stopped again.

"What's wrong?" he asked.

"Just making sure Foghorn isn't around."

She finally grew brave enough to look up at him. Curiosity lit up his eyes, and she admitted this was better. There was still a tension between them, but talking had been good for them. It was the most time they'd spent alone with each other all week.

"Foghorn?" he asked.

"Leghorn." She moved toward the stables again. "My dad got this idea in his head that the ranch needed farm fresh chickens. It was right after his heart attack, and he got on a health kick. Anyway, he bought a bunch of eggs, hatched them up from babies, then set them free to forage on the ranch." She shook her head. "The darn things have been terrorizing the place ever since."

When she risked glancing up at him again she thought she saw a smile. The tension in her shoulders started to ease. This was good. Humor. A balm to the soul.

"They tore up my aunt's garden earlier this year. Scratched it out of existence. She told my dad she was going to eat them all."

Yup. That was definitely a smile starting to crack the surface of his stony face.

"Well, one of them turned out to be a rooster." She paused in front of the stables. This time of day the setting sun was blocked by the mountains to the west, but there was enough ambient light that she could tell he'd had some experience with roosters. His lips twitched.

"Yeah." She shook her head. "It's part of why I don't come down here very often anymore. Well, that and my dad. I've been calling him Hannibal the Cannibal." It was her turn to smile. "If you see him, run."

"Duly noted."

They turned back to the stable, the smell of pine shavings hanging in the air. One of her family members must have raked the barn aisle earlier, probably Flynn.

"This place is really something," she heard him say.

"My dad and uncle had it built."

"I thought it was a villa when I first drove in."

She smiled. "A lot of people think that. It's actually taller than the house I grew up in." She looked up at a large window. "We keep hay up there. Office at the end. Show horses are in the barn. Ranch and rodeo horses are kept outside."

They moved toward a stall on her right, a bright-eyed mare peeking her head up, a piece of hay sticking out of her mouth.

"Hey there, old girl," she said softly.

There was nothing more soothing to her than the smell of horse. She opened the stall door, slowly sliding the door to the right, Scarlett taking a step toward her.

She suddenly found herself teary-eyed.

"How are you?" she asked, walking up to the mare, hand outstretched. "It's been a while, hasn't it?"

Why had she stayed away so long? Jayden wondered. She shouldn't have let her dad scare her away. Or used that damned rooster as an excuse.

Her old friend clearly recognized her, forgetting her food for a moment so she could give Jayden a good sniff. She laughed, having forgotten Colby's presence for a moment.

"Looking for treats?" she asked, the mare sniffing her pockets. "I'm afraid I don't have any." She scratched the mare's jaw. "I'll go get you one in a moment."

"She definitely seems to have the kind of personality we're always looking for."

She nodded. Scarlett lifted her head, curious about the man who'd come in behind her.

"She does. I think she'd make an amazing therapy horse. Plus, it'd be great to work with her again."

Because she felt guilty. Riding had once been such a huge part of her life, but she hadn't even brought Paisley down in here in weeks. Aunt Crystal was always the one letting her daughter pet the horses. And all because of her pride.

"Let me show you Sparky next."

"Sparky?"

"He's in the last stall on the left."

Colby didn't move for a moment. She froze, her pulse skittering off, because she'd noticed it, too.

It was back.

The sexual tension that refused to go away. She gave Colby as wide a berth as possible, latching the stall door closed and turning toward Sparky's stall.

And that was when she saw him. A two-legged demon with white feathers.

"Colby, watch out."

The rooster ran at him like Road Runner in a Looney Tunes cartoon. Colby turned. The rooster took flight. Colby narrowly missed being spurred, his cry of "Hey" startling the horses in the barn, but the man had the reflexes of a cat, because in the next instant he'd snatched off his hat, tossing it at Foghorn like a Frisbee, which made Leghorn squawk in protest and leave just as quickly as he'd come.

Jayden could only stare, and then her shoulders began to shake.

"Damn thing," he said, marching forward to pick

up his hat, slapping it against his leg to clean it off. "It tried to kill me."

She collapsed against Scarlett's stall. She couldn't help it. It must have been the stress of the past week or maybe a release of the tension in the air, but suddenly she couldn't breathe, she laughed so hard.

Colby just stared.

She doubled over. Dear goodness, she had tears coming out of her eyes.

"The look on your face," she gasped out. "You must have thought you were back in a war zone."

When she straightened again, he hadn't moved. Her laughter faded. Why was he looking at her like that?

"I've never seen you laugh like that before."

Because she rarely ever did, not lately, not with work and school and raising a kid and trying to make ends meet and trying to make rent and keep the power on and make her car payments and her sorrow over her dad.

"It's been a long time since I've done that," she admitted.

Her heart began to pound. He wasn't moving. Neither was she.

It happened again.

The electricity danced in the air. It sizzled between them, making her forget that she'd sworn to stop thinking about their kiss. That was all she could think about right now. The way he'd touched her. How it'd felt to have his lips press up against her own.

"Why?"

She had to blink. Had to think about his question. "No time."

He took a step toward her. Goose bumps sprouted on her arms. His stare was like a physical touch, one that made her hyperaware of the fact that he was a man and she was a woman.

"It's been hard for you, hasn't it?"

She nodded. "I'd be lying if I told you it's been easy."

He took another step toward her. Her skin began to tingle.

"Not that my aunt and uncle wouldn't give me the shirts off their backs if I asked."

One more step. "But you never ask."

She shook her head, perhaps a bit too fast. She felt dizzy all of a sudden, or maybe that was the result of him being so near, of the way the smell of him drifted on a current of air.

"I never wanted to put them in that position." Her voice sounded strange to her ears. "If my dad found out, it would put a strain on their relationship. I had to ask my aunt and uncle to help me make rent last month. It killed me."

He was inches away now, and she knew, she just knew, that they would kiss again, that they could no more stay away from each other than rain could fall toward the sky.

"You shouldn't have to take care of yourself." His head lowered. "You should be pampered and cherished and made love to every night."

She gasped. He gently pulled her toward him, and she let him, God help her, she let him pull her up against his hard body, her eyes closing as her head fell back so he could kiss her.

The world tilted. Her feet lifted off the ground. Or at least, that was what it felt like. The same dizzying sensation, like stepping off a curb that she didn't see, the same disorientation, the same need to right herself, overcame her. The only way to anchor herself was to hold him. She felt him tense for a second, thought he might stop, but he must have lost his battle with common sense, too, because suddenly his arms slipped around her, his mouth pressing against her own so that she did the most reckless thing of all. She opened her mouth. His tongue slipped inside, and he tasted like perfection, a salty sweetness that spread warmth through her soul.

His hand dropped down to her side, and she flinched from his touch as if it hurt, but it didn't hurt, far from it. Pleasure. That was all she felt. His fingers were like the jolt from an outlet, a jolt that traveled through her body and made her moan. And then he tensed again, and she realized he was moving against her, pushing her so that her back was up against a wall. He lifted her slightly, and she wrapped her legs around him. He groaned. She tipped her head to the side, trying to tell him without words what she wanted, and he must have heard her silent cry because he started to move against her. She arched into him, thought she heard him moan when their bodies touched at that most intimate of junctures, and she wanted more. So much more.

His hand slid beneath the T-shirt she wore. No special clothes for him, she'd told herself. No dressing up. And now she reaped the rewards because it was easy for him to cup her breasts, to pull her bra down, to lift the shirt so his mouth could…

She groaned. Dear Lord, if he kept this up she'd lose herself right here and now.

A rooster crowed.

They both froze, both turned, both spotted the feathered white devil standing at the end of the barn. It eyed them in the same way a shark would eye its next meal, and from nowhere came the urge to laugh again. It was wrong. What they were doing couldn't happen, but then he was laughing and slowly letting her down, and it should have been a disappointment because she'd wanted what his mouth and his hands and his body promised her, but his smile and the soft sound he made when he laughed, oh, it did things to her. Did things that made her want to revert to the wild and crazy young woman she once was…before Paisley. Before disappointing her dad. Before she'd had to pull herself up by the bootstraps and support herself.

Her feet touched the ground. She raised her hand and placed it against the side of his face, and his laughter faded.

"It's been a long time for you, too, hasn't it?" she asked.

He fixed her bra, pulled her shirt down, but he didn't let her go. "Longer than you know."

She almost shook her head. No. She did know.

Chapter 13

He didn't want to let her go.

Her eyes held him like riptide, their color as blue as the water on a Caribbean beach. He saw things in that gaze, things he'd never thought to see in a woman's eyes again, only this time it was different. This time it made him think things no sane man with his kind of hang-ups should be thinking.

"We should go."

His body still hummed in response to what they'd almost done. His heart tapped his chest in the same way the stock of an automatic rifle hit him when it fired. He wanted to keep on kissing her, but that damn rooster was still nearby.

She must have been thinking the same thing, because her lips tipped up in wry amusement, but when their gazes met again, some of the heat between them still lingered.

"Let me show you Sparky."

He moved back, reluctantly, because he knew the moment their bodies parted it would start to fade, this crazy, unimaginable attraction, and in its place would follow the ice-cold touch of sanity.

She stepped away. He moved back even farther, and it was as if he could suddenly breathe, as if he'd been underwater holding his breath and now he'd broken the surface again, his face cooling, his mind clear of the grogginess that came with lack of air.

She kept walking. He hung back, scooped up a rock from the barn aisle, lobbed it at the renegade rooster, who squawked in outrage and flew off.

When he turned back to her he wanted to hurry and catch up to her, to say a million things at once, and also nothing at all. She seemed to be gathering herself, too, as she took a deep breath and squared her shoulders. She headed toward another stall at the end of the row with the same determination of a soldier who'd just been mustered.

"We need to talk." He had to pull the words up from deep inside him, because they didn't want to be said. "That shouldn't have happened."

She stared at the horse behind the wrought iron bars of its stall. The bay horse eyed them curiously. He watched her lift a hand, place it between the bars, the horse coming forward and sniffing her. He used one of the same bars to hold himself up, clutching it and leaning into it, as he peered down at her.

"You don't need to say anything." She pretended an interest in the horse. "I'm just as aware of all the reasons why this would never work out as you are."

He clutched the bar tighter. "Not all the reasons."

Something in his voice must have caught her attention. Her eyes caught his own, and he began to sink down into the depth of them again before he caught himself and drew back.

"I'd be no good for you." He sucked in a breath of air, his throat starting to constrict. "There's things…"

Why was it so hard to tell her?

"…things going on up here." He tapped his head. "Things that make me impossible to love."

Love? When had love entered into this? Why the hell had he even mentioned the word?

Dusky light poured in through the open door in front of her, brushing her face with the delicate hues of pinks and golds. She looked as delicate as a doll, her face so small compared to him he could cup the whole thing in a palm, her lashes so thick and so dark they were like the edges of a butterfly's wings, their surface painted a dazzling blue. Those eyes filled with confusion. He told himself to leave it alone, that he'd said enough.

"I'm not the same as I was before," he said, for some reason compelled to explain. "When I returned from over there, I just…"

He'd never spoken to anyone about this before, not even Liz.

"I was just different. Liz saw it. My dad saw it, too. They both did. I think in some ways I drove her into his arms—"

"No." She clutched the hand he'd been using to prop himself up. "Whatever you might think, there was no excuse for that."

God help him, he wanted to kiss her again. Instead, he grasped the iron bar as tight as he could, rooting himself to the earth, his other hand balling into a fist.

"I changed over there, Jayden, and not for the better. It's hard to blame Liz when I know…"

Her eyes scanned his, first one and then the other, as if seeking to put together truth by finding the answers in his eyes. He almost lifted his hand, the free one, and smoothed a lock of black hair off her face. The pale pink sky gilded the silky strands reds and golds. She could not have been more beautiful to him in that moment than any other woman in the world. He understood then what it meant to have someone take your breath away, because he felt as if he couldn't breathe.

"What happened?"

He didn't want to tell her. He feared if she heard the truth he might never see softness in her eyes again. But wasn't that what he wanted? Shouldn't he be pushing her away? For her own good. And yet…he couldn't.

"Nothing I want to share." He let go of the bar, turned to face the horse. "Nothing you need to hear."

She didn't say anything. It was her move next. God help him, and if she touched him, if she showed him any sort of kindness, he'd kiss her again, and this time he doubted he'd be able to stop.

"I suppose it doesn't matter anyway," he heard her say. "We're kidding ourselves if we think this could ever work out."

Just like he'd been kidding himself when he'd come back from overseas, thinking his guilt and his shame and his terrible mood swings would fade with time. They hadn't.

"Tell me about Sparky," he said, nodding at the horse.

She peeked up at him, held his gaze for a moment,

and he could tell she'd seize the change of subject with both hands.

"What do you want to know?"

She avoided him the rest of the night, easy to do in a large crowd of people. Her family was loud and boisterous and kept Colby entertained, and so she told herself she could ignore him, and she did…for the most part.

"He seems like a nice man," her brother Maverick said as they both watched Colby leave the party. "Flynn must be thrilled he'll take Sparky and Scarlett off his hands."

She told herself not to watch him go, but the veranda leached light from the interior of the home, giving her a perfect view of him as he stood and said his goodbyes. His gaze connected with her own. It was the visual equivalent of being zapped by a cattle prod.

"I'm just glad they're going to a good home, especially Scarlett."

Beneath Maverick's cowboy hat, his eyes narrowed with a smile. "You always did have a soft spot for that horse."

Maverick was in charge of her father's cattle operation, which was a job unto itself. Horses were a piece of equipment to him, a means to an end, and so he'd never gotten close to them like she had. Now dogs… His cattle dog, Sadie, meant the world to him. She sat off to the side of the family, her eyes trained on her human.

"I'm glad it worked out," Jax said from across the table.

"Me, too," said Flynn from all the way from the other end.

"You think Dad will be okay with it?"

Everyone grew quiet for a moment, and she realized her father was the elephant in the room. Did they know she'd tried to talk to him earlier in the week?

"He'll be fine with it," said Uncle Bob. "He knows those two horses will be better served at Dark Horse Ranch."

The light from a citronella candle flickered across the faces at the table. Her aunt had retired for the night. Paisley slept on a blanket not far from where she sat. Tomorrow would be a busy day, and she knew she would need to leave soon, but she waited until she heard Colby's truck make its way down the driveway before announcing, "I should probably leave, too."

Her boss caught her gaze.

She'd gotten to know him a little better tonight, had heard all about his military contracting firm and the adorable story about how he'd met his wife, and stories the rest of her family seemed familiar with.

He still intimidated the hell out of her, and so when she stood and he said almost instantly, "Jayden, can I talk to you for a sec?" she tensed.

What had she done? Dear Lord in heaven, he hadn't seen them down at the barn, had he? No. The rooster would have been after him if he'd been nearby.

"Sure." She glanced down at Paisley, still out cold. She had a feeling whatever he wanted to say to her, he'd prefer to do so in private, so she retreated to a picnic bench off to the side of the veranda, one shielded by the branches of an old oak tree, the leaves concealing the stars above.

"What's up?" she asked, her hands splaying flat on the wooden slats so that she could feel the initials her brother Shane had carved into the seat over a year ago. "S+K." Shane plus Kait.

Jax took a seat next to her, and it was dark, but not so dark that she couldn't make out his face, his gray hair more silvered by the moon behind them.

"First of all, I just wanted to tell you how much we love having you at the ranch." He leaned forward, rested his arms on his legs, hands clasped. "You're doing a great job."

The breath she released deflated her shoulders. "Thank you."

"But you looked a little weird when you came back from the barn. Colby wasn't being difficult again, was he?"

Damn. She'd known it would be something like that. She'd tried to paste a smile on her face, had known she'd failed miserably. Colby had it easy. His face always had a stony countenance, and so he'd looked normal.

"I was just out of breath from the climb up the drive," she hedged.

He didn't say anything, but that didn't surprise her. The man had a lie detector for ears. She pitied his kids.

"Look. I'm going to be honest. I've been worried about Colby for a while now. The ranch is his life. He never goes out. Never calls home, at least not that I know of. Never gets visitors. Never goes anywhere." He frowned. "He's a lot like Bryan in a way. I was hoping the two of them would connect somehow, maybe help each other, but that's a whole other problem."

They'd both closed themselves off.

I changed over there, Jayden, and not for the better.
But at least Bryan's family wanted to help him. Colby

had been betrayed. Nobody had been there for him, probably not in a long, long time.

"Anyway." Jax looked like a man who'd walked through a graveyard and been chased out by ghosts. "I just wanted to make sure you know that he might come off as cold and distant at times, but he's a good guy. Don't let him get you down."

He hadn't been cold earlier. Not at all.

She had to look away, but not before she caught a glimpse of sadness in her boss's eyes, that and something else. It was as if he understood what Colby had been through in a way that only someone who'd battled their own demons could. For the first time she wondered what Jax had been through in the past. What demons did her boss carry from his own time in the military? No wonder he wanted her to understand Colby. It probably drove him to help his friend Bryan, too.

He stood, looked down at her. "His bark is worse than his bite, Jayden. Be patient with him."

He walked away, his footfalls muffled by the damp grass and a dusting of leaves that coated the ground.

Be patient.

She didn't want to be patient. She wanted to put Jax's words from her head, to keep the barriers up, because when Colby kissed her it was like clinging to the back of an unbroken colt, unpredictable and terrifying and yet when the dust settled and you started moving as one, so perfectly wonderful that it brought tears to your eyes.

And that scared her to death.

Chapter 14

"You know, you should probably just jump her."

Colby snapped his head around, his arm freezing in the midst of brushing Bentley. Bryan Vance. Just what he needed.

"I mean, I've been watching you two for the better part of a week now, and it's all getting kind of old. And today…today you haven't stopped staring at her since you tied that damn horse up."

He slowly turned to face the man. He hadn't shaved. Not in days. He'd started to take on the appearance of a mountain man. Hair mussed, the gray more pronounced because of its longer length.

"Can I help you, Mr. Vance?"

Inside the arena, Jayden worked with Dylan and three other people. Derrick, their ranch manager, had finally returned. The older man worked on the hinge of one of the arena gates, fixing a pesky squeak. Volun-

teers led the horses the disabled veterans rode, Jayden
in the middle calling out each exercise. She'd just asked
them to pat their head and rub circles on their belly, and
there'd been a burst of laughter. That was what made
him look. The grizzled army veterans might think it a
funny childhood game, but it really did help with hand-
eye coordination, opening neural pathways and increas-
ing motor skills.

"I don't need help. You're the one who needs help.
Mooning after that woman."

Colby held on to his patience by the thinnest of
threads. "You riding today?"

"No." Bryan wheeled his chair toward him.

For over a week now they'd been trying to coax Bryan
to ride. He'd resisted at every turn. Jax had even been
called in at one point. The two had retired to Bryan's
cabin. Colby had no idea what had been said, but his
boss's friend was still a no-show every morning. He
ate. He slept. Sometimes they'd see him wheeling himself around the property, but that was the extent of his
therapy.

You can't help those who don't want to be helped.

"Is there something else I can do for you, then?" His
movements echoed the terseness of his words, Bentley
lifting her head, he brushed her so hard. He instantly
softened his touch. Damn the man. His frustration had
translated to the horse. Or maybe it was a different type
of frustration, one born from having to watch Jayden
all morning. He didn't know. Didn't care. Or so he told
himself.

"Nope." Bryan's word sounded almost chipper. "I'm
just here for the entertainment. Kind of fun to watch a

bunch of clowns playing kindergarten games on horseback."

Colby swiped a little too hard again. "Yeah, well, at least they're trying." He stopped, switched the brush to his other hand. "Years from now you'll look back at this moment and realize things could have been different. Instead you'll be that old man in a wheelchair that all the kids are scared of."

It wasn't like him to be so ugly to a guest, but his frustration with his life had spilled over into his professional life.

"Sounds good to me." Bryan rolled his chair forward and then back again. "At least I'm not afraid to admit what I am."

And there he went trying to bait him again, but it wouldn't work. Instead Colby tossed the brush into the box and headed for the tack room, returning with a saddle and pad a moment later, the metal end of the girth dragging on the ground. He didn't care.

"The difference between you and me is I have your best interest at heart, whereas you only care about yourself."

"What's wrong with that?"

Colby tossed the saddle pad over Bentley's back. "I'll tell you what's wrong with that. You're not alone in this. You have friends and a family who care if you get better. And a whole team of people with your best interest at heart. And instead of thinking of them, you're too busy wallowing in self-pity to care."

Bryan's brows lowered. "You have no idea what I'm dealing with."

The saddle landed on Bentley's back with a soft *thud*. "You might be surprised."

Silence. Colby presumed it was nose-out-of-joint kind of quiet, the kind of muteness caused by impotent fury. But when he switched sides to start girthing up, he happened to glance over at Bryan. He was studying him intently.

"What branch?"

"Excuse me?"

"What branch of the military were you in?"

So he'd finally figured it out. "Army."

"Special Forces?"

He tugged on the girth strap. "Once upon a time."

"How many years were you in?"

"Eight." The leather strap made a snapping sound, he pulled on it so tight. "And before you ask, medical discharge."

He let that sink in as he finished, and when he was done, he stopped in front of Bryan. "I was part of a cleanup team in Iraq tasked with finding and eliminating rebel strongholds. We were about three days out when we became separated from our convoy. Freak sandstorm. Too far out to get back in time." He refocused on Bentley, checked to make sure he had the saddle in the right position. "Found a place to wait it out, but what we didn't realize is we were in the middle of a nest of Iraqi insurgents. Weather cleared up. Both sides opened fire. We were outmanned and outgunned. I tried my best to get my unit out unscathed. Couldn't do it."

This next part was hard, so hard he had to clutch the saddle for support. He took a deep breath.

"I watched my men get picked off one by one." He shook his head, closed his eyes, remembering the sound, the screams, the smell. Some days he would swear he could still smell the acrid stench of gunpowder. "I was wounded. Bad. Rescue team tried to get to me. I say *tried* because they had to turn back the first time. Taking on too much fire. I had to sit there, my men dead all around me, wondering if I should just take my gun and end it for myself. Their second try they got me out, but I sat there for six days. Six goddamn days."

He turned, something catching his attention. Jayden. She stood just off the rail, listening, and there was such a look of horror on her face that he had to turn away. Well, it was about time she learned the whole ugly truth. Maybe she'd realize what a loser he was. A strong man, a *good* man, wouldn't have thought about taking his own life.

He turned back to Bryan. "So I know exactly what you've been through, asshole. I've been through worse than you. But you know what? Who cares? What I *do* know is you're done. You either ride today or you're going home. I'm sick of wasting my time and yours."

Bryan stared. Colby didn't give a damn. He walked Bentley back into her stall, where he'd tie her up until it was time for her to go to work. When he came back out, Bryan had already wheeled himself out of the barn, his arms pumping with such ferocity it was like he was trying to wheel himself all the way back to his home state.

Colby probably shouldn't have spoken so harshly.

He caught Jayden's gaze, but only for an instant, a horse blocking his view for a moment, and he was grateful for the temporary loss of eye contact, because he couldn't look at her. He didn't want to see what was in her eyes. Probably disappointment. Maybe even disgust. Nothing more than he felt for himself.

Damn it.

So he turned away, went about his task of getting the

other horses ready, putting Bryan and his troubles with Jayden out of his mind, at least until he came face-to-face with her as her lesson ended. It was chaotic then, however, as they worked with veterans on dismounting before they headed off to lunch, their next batch of riders arriving one by one.

And Bryan.

Colby froze near the front of the arena and the ramp they used to mount guests on horseback and where they told everyone to meet. All the veterans and a few of their volunteers watched Bryan approach. The sound of clopping hooves coming down the barn aisle preceded Jayden as she emerged leading Annie. She stopped, too.

"Well," Bryan snapped. "What are we waiting for?"

Jayden fought the urge to cry.

Colby's story. What he'd been through... No wonder he kept pulling away from her. The guilt she'd heard in his voice...

But she needed to focus. Bryan needed them now. The man grumbled as they hoisted him onto Beau, and it was lucky that the other three guests were ex-military, too, because the man could curse like a sailor. And they were also fortunate that their guests had a good enough handle on guiding a horse they didn't need a volunteer on one side of them like Bryan did, something else he complained about as they led him away from the ramp and toward Derrick, who held the gate he'd been working on open for them.

"You can take your lunch now," Colby said.

His look was the same as it'd been earlier, full of shame and maybe even anger. Angry? At himself? Her? Bryan?

"Actually, I would rather stay if that's okay." Even though a part of her would like to leave as much as he wanted her gone. "You're a little shorthanded anyway."

"Can we get on with this?"

They both turned toward Bryan. Jayden lifted a brow. Colby swung away.

Penny, one of their volunteers, guided Beau toward the arena. They'd secured Bryan to a special saddle, one designed for quadriplegics, with a chair-like back and belts that were secured around a patient's waist and special stirrups that would keep his feet in place.

Colby moved to the center of the ring. He would be ringmaster for this round. The other three vets, all men younger than Bryan, smiled as they filed one by one into the arena. Not Bryan. He had the same look on his face as an army major who'd lost a battle, and maybe in some ways that was how he viewed his therapy.

"Okay," Colby called. "Everyone circle around me. We're going to stay at this end of the arena, and the first thing we're going to do is our warm-up exercises. Does everyone remember how to do those?"

"Try to touch your toes." Jayden smiled up at Bryan. "I'll make sure you don't fall."

"I can't even feel my damn toes. How the hell do you expect me to know if I'm touching them?"

She forced her smile to stay in place. "I'll tell you if you've done it right."

Bryan eyed her like she was the simplest form of life on earth. "Come on. Try it." She increased the wattage of her smile. "It's good for strengthening your core."

"Why? So I'll have abs of steel for the ladies? No, thanks. I doubt anyone will be looking at me in a damn wheelchair."

He would try the patience of a saint. But mixed in with her frustration she felt a deep vein of sympathy for the man. He was clearly in pain, both physically and mentally, and even though he was a colossal pain in the rear, she empathized with him. "Penny," she said to their volunteer, "why don't you just let him go?"

Penny glanced back at her in surprise. "Excuse me, Miss Gillian?"

She stepped away from Bryan. "Tie the lead around Beau's neck. We're going to let Bryan decide where he wants to go."

"What's going on?" Colby called.

Penny had pulled Beau to a stop off to the side. She helped him secure the lead rope.

"Bryan doesn't want to do any of the exercises, so I thought we'd just let him ride around on his own."

Colby signaled for the other men to stop. He crooked a finger at her. She hated being summoned like that, resisted the urge to do the same thing back, but they should probably discuss things out of Bryan's earshot.

"You can't just turn him loose," he hissed when she walked up to him.

"Actually, Colby, that's exactly what I'm going to do. I'm going to turn him loose without a spotter or anyone controlling the horse. I'm going to let him be the one in control. Beau will be fine," she said, reading the look in his eyes. "That horse wouldn't harm a fly."

"He might lose his balance."

"He might do that even with someone standing by his side. We should let him go. Let him figure it out. Lord knows nothing else we've done so far has worked."

"I'm not getting any younger," Bryan called in a sing-song voice.

"You know, for a man in his thirties, he can sure act like my three-year-old," she grumbled.

Colby stared down at her, and the carefully blank expression had faded. In his eyes she saw some of the same desperation she felt, a need to help someone that was as intrinsic as it was to breathe. It was part of what drew her to him, she admitted. Part of the reason why, even now, standing in the middle of an arena, she felt the need to touch him, to grab his big hand and squeeze and tell him it would be all right.

"Let him go, Penny," he called, motioning the volunteer over. "Bryan, you're on your own. The rest of you guys keep circling. This time I want you to reach behind you and try to touch your horse's tail."

"What am I supposed to do with this?" Bryan motioned toward the reins Walter had just handed him. He had to hold them tight, which was probably a challenge with his damaged hands, but good for him. "My hands are no good for anything."

"You'll figure it out."

But Colby's eyes conveyed his uncertainty about her plan. He rolled the dice anyway, and it meant the world to her that he trusted her judgment. When Paisley had turned three she'd drawn her first picture, handing it to her with pride in her eyes, and Jayden had felt such a flood of emotion it'd filled her eyes with tears. She experienced the same influx of emotion now.

"This will work," she said softly.

It had to work. Something had to get through to the man.

"Hello," Bryan said. "You two just going to let me stand here all day?"

"Move your hand in the direction you want to go."

Jayden forced herself to not reach for the reins to show him. "Pull back if you want to stop."

"*Stop?* Hard to stop when you're standing still."

"Cluck, like this." Jayden clicked her tongue against the roof of her mouth. "That's Beau's cue to move forward."

"I'm not going to cluck like a damn chicken. You guys can just take me out of here right now. I'm done with this. Done with it all. And I'm going to sue you for putting my life in danger. I don't have use of my hands, and you've just left me standing here."

"Your hands work just fine," Colby yelled right back. "Well enough to guide Beau."

Jayden didn't know if it was Bryan's yelling or Colby's or the divine hand of God, but Beau started to walk forward.

"Hey, hey." He clutched the saddle horn, reins slack in his hands. "It's moving. Tell him to stop."

"His name is Beau." Colby's voice conveyed his own impatience. "And Jayden told you how to stop. Pull back on the reins. Or move your hand to the left or right if you want to go somewhere."

That was exactly what Bryan did. He jerked the reins with such force Jayden wondered if his hands were really as weak as he made them out to be. Beau thrust his head up. Lord love the blue roan gelding, though, because he didn't get mad, just pushed his head down so that the reins were nearly jerked out of Bryan's hands, forcing him to grab for them. Beau started heading for the gate.

"There, see. We're leaving."

The other three riders in the arena had gone quiet, eyes wide. They seemed to know what was going on, following Colby's instructions while Bryan ranted and raved the whole way.

Beau stopped at the gate.

"See. Even the horse wants out. Let me out of here," he told Derrick.

"Not until the hour's up," Colby said. "If you don't want to sit there like a bump on a log, I suggest you make that horse turn and follow the other riders around. I know from your file that you know how to ride. Quit your bellyaching and move. You're in the way right there."

Beneath the rectangular patches of sunlight beaming down from the roof, Jayden did her best to ignore Bryan's frustrated grunts. Derrick had stopped repairing the gate and stood watching. Bryan jerked the reins again, Beau doing the same thing as before, but Bryan was ready for him, and this time Bryan took the end of the reins and slapped the horse.

Beau took off at a trot. Jayden ran toward the pair, but Bryan's "Hey" and then "Whoa" did the trick. Beau walked again. She stopped.

"That was great," said one of the other vets, a blond twentysomething named Seth. "I want to try to trot."

"Does everyone want to do that?" Colby asked the group.

"I didn't do it on purpose."

But everyone ignored Bryan, and after a chorus of "Let's go" and "Yes" and "I'm game," the volunteers all took up the slack in their lead ropes and pulled the horses forward. Seth started to laugh; one of the other veterans cried out in surprise before he, too, started to laugh.

Beau began to trot.

"Whoa. Whoa," Bryan cried.

The horse didn't listen. He was used to following along behind his pals, and Bryan was too busy clutching the saddle horn to pull back. When he made a full lap around the arena, he tugged the reins to the right and headed for the opposite end. Jayden glanced at Colby. They both watched him go. They pretended not to, of course, but they both saw Bryan tug the reins to the left, Beau heading off the rail, toward the middle, Bryan moving the reins to the right next. All the while he kept on trotting.

"Okay, everyone, stop and then change directions."

Jayden helped direct traffic, so to speak, as horses and riders turned around. They resumed their exercises, Bryan now at the opposite end, walking, but Jayden noticed he turned around, too. It was like watching someone drive a vehicle. Left. Right. Walk. Trot. Turn around. Bryan directed the horse, and she could tell he grew more and more comfortable with each passing minute. They let him go and, when the hour was up, left the arena gate open so he could let himself out.

Bryan didn't leave. He kept working with Beau.

Jayden turned to Colby, and she knew he'd spy the hope in her eyes, but she didn't dare voice her thoughts out loud for fear Bryan would overhear. They went about the business of getting everyone dismounted.

"Can you and Derrick handle getting the horses and the tack?" Colby asked. "I think I'm going to take him out on a trail. I want him to feel what it's like to have legs again, even if they're horse legs."

"Yes, of course."

He held her gaze for a moment longer. "You were right to trust your instincts, Jayden." She saw gratitude in the depths of his eyes, his face softening in a way she'd only ever seen when he kissed her. Had they been anything other than coworkers, he might have touched her then, and she tensed out of hope that he might. But he didn't, just turned away, and her shoulders lost the battle with anticipation.

She'd wanted him to kiss her. She dropped her gaze to the ground so that nobody could see just how much.

And that was the moment Jayden realized she wanted so much more than friendship from him.

Chapter 15

It'd been a good day. A remarkable day, really, Colby thought.

"Are you up there?"

Except for that. Jayden. The sound of her voice was like a kick to the solar plexus, and even though he wanted, oh, how he wanted, to ignore her, he knew he couldn't. Today was payday. Time to hand her a paycheck.

"Come on up," he called back, sliding the envelope with her first two weeks of wages toward the edge of his desk, as far away from him as possible. Hopefully she'd pick it up and leave.

"You know, there are days when I could cheerfully take the elevator." She entered his office, her words like sunshine and happiness. Or maybe that was just the way she made him feel. "Today kicked my butt even with all of Derrick's help."

She didn't grab the envelope, which sat in obvious contrast to his desk, the white paper very nearly hanging off the edge. Instead she settled herself in the seat opposite him, forcing him to look up and study her as he'd done that first day she'd come to work.

Only two weeks ago? It felt like a lifetime.

"I like Derrick," she volunteered. "He's a little older than I expected, but I think that's because my brothers manage Gillian Ranch and they're only a few years older than myself, so I guess I just figured he'd be about the same age."

"He's a hard worker. That's all that matters."

"Yes, of course. I noticed that today." She smiled. "Is it always going to be this busy?"

He had to swallow to get his vocal cords to work. "For the next few months. And wait until wedding season starts when we're working around all that and more. You'll be glad when the winter months arrive. Things will slow down then."

She tipped her head so that her ponytail fell over a shoulder. "I had no idea it would be this much work."

That was why he loved it so much. Never had time to think. He'd been able to close himself off to the world. And then she'd arrived and changed everything. Now he sat in his office, very nearly in pain, he ached for her so badly, and it was all he could do to keep his gaze from sliding over her face. If he started studying the gentle curve of her jaw, or admiring how the light turned her eyes the color of first-place ribbons, or how her lips looked as if she'd recently licked them, he knew she'd see some of what he thought on his face. His leg began to quiver, he had tensed up so much.

"There's your check." He turned away, pretending

to focus on the laptop to his left. "You should get your direct-deposit form back to me."

Because sitting in a closed space with her was hell. He could smell her. Cherry blossoms on a spring day. She tasted as sweet as the fruit, too, and the memory of her straddling him, of the way her warmth had cradled him and heated him and made him want to...

"See you tomorrow."

He couldn't have been more overt in his dismissal of her, but she didn't take the hint. He hoped he hid his sigh of impatience, because he didn't want her to know what she did to him. So he steeled himself, lifted his gaze to meet her eyes.

"Was there something else?" he asked.

Her eyes were so big. It looked like he could dive into them.

"I, ah..."

He saw her chest rise and fall. She wore a white long-sleeved T-shirt, and his imagination went crazy when he thought about what might be beneath the pale fabric.

"I just wanted to say good job with Bryan today." She slowly scooped the check off his desk. "It was genius to take him on a trail ride. He seemed like a different person afterward."

For the love of all that's holy. Stop the small talk and leave.

"You did good, too." He had to give her that. If she hadn't come up with the idea of turning Bryan loose and letting him throw a fit and thereby forcing him to work with Beau, who knew if they ever would have gotten through to the man. And then later, when they'd gotten back from the trail ride, the man had actually thanked him.

"I—" he had to cough to get his voice to work right "—I appreciate you working through your lunch."

"My pleasure."

His hands had started to shake. He wanted to open up an email, a document, a file, anything to keep them busy.

"Colby, about what you told Bryan—"

"No." The word was the verbal equivalent of pistol fire. "No. We do *not* need to talk about that."

Ever.

The word was the silent punctuation at the end of a sentence. She stared at him, and something in her eyes changed. Her brows lifted ever so slightly, and he knew she'd finally put two and two together, that she realized he held on to control by the thinnest of threads.

"I'm so sorry."

She stood, so quickly that she dropped her check. She made a grab for it, but it disappeared beneath his desk, landing close to his foot. She moved to come around to his side of the desk, but he didn't want her coming close, so he ducked down and scooped the envelope up.

She stood over him. He reared back in his chair and thrust the check out. She didn't move.

The silence in the room was like that before a bomb blast, the total quieting of sound and air, as if a million people had inhaled at once, sucking the world into stillness, and he knew he was doomed.

"Colby."

He closed his eyes. It was a move of self-defense. If he didn't see her, the tension would ease. Maybe she'd take it as a silent signal to go away.

"I don't know what to do."

Her words sounded as agonized as he felt. His hands

found the arms of his office chair, giving them something to hold on to other than her.

Jayden.

Never had he wanted anything as badly as he wanted
the woman in front of him. He knew then what it meant
to be consumed by desire. He was a shoreline pounded
by waves, his desire to keep away from her eaten away
bit by bit until there was nothing left of his willpower.

And then she took his hand.

He released a breath as if he'd been underwater too
long. Her thumb gently caressed the back of his hand.
He wondered if she thought she needed to tame him,
if she sensed the wild animal she roused within him,
hoped to soothe the beast with her gentle touch. It didn't
work.

His eyes opened. He saw it then. Longing. Hope.
Desire.

"We shouldn't." It was all he could think to say.

"I know."

"If someone finds out."

Yes, her eyes seemed to say. *Yes, I know.*

But she was as helpless to fight the force of their attraction as he was. He saw that, too.

"Maybe just this once?" she offered softly.

It was that moment of insanity when someone suggested something completely outrageous and that you
knew was wrong, but at the same time it seemed perfectly sane. *In*sane. That was what this was. *Insanity.*

He tugged on her hand, pulled her down to him, and
she went willingly, her mouth opening at the same time
she straddled his lap.

Dear God.

The cry echoed through his head. He welcomed that

open mouth, swept his tongue inside so he could taste her once again, guided her so that her hot warmth covered the ache in his groin. But the crash of their bodies was nothing compared to the sweet release of holding her. She made him think things, thoughts he'd never had, primal male urges to protect her, shield her and keep her safe.

He'd failed at that once before.

He started to draw back. She wouldn't let him, pulled him even closer, changed the angle of her head, kissed him in a way that seemed to reach deep into his core, and he forgot about his past and the men he'd been sworn to protect and the families he'd let down. His mind could think about one thing. Sucking in the sweet essence that was Jayden, the insides of her mouth as hot as the ache in his groin, her tongue as soft as silk.

She came up for air. He gasped at his sudden ability to breathe. She still held his head, still peered down at him, her eyes soft and full of wanton desire.

"I want you, Colby Kotch," she said softly. "I want you even though my wanting scares the hell out of me."

Yes. He knew how she felt.

His chest rose and fell like a hunted man's, and when he tried to talk, his voice sounded harsh, guttural. "I want you, too."

The flame in her eyes flickered. "Then take me to your bed."

She knew where his room was, had noted its location that first day when he'd given her a tour, and she heard voices coming from down the hall as they passed, but she wouldn't have cared if the boogeyman had come tearing down the hall and tried to scare her away.

She was doing this.

It didn't matter what she risked, or that it might affect their jobs, and that at some point, sanity would return and she'd have to live with the ramifications of what they were about to do. All that mattered was the here and now, and she wanted him.

Here.

Now.

His door was open, and when it closed behind her, he turned and faced her and she looked into his eyes and she saw it then, the uncertainty that hid beneath the heat in his eyes. She'd seen it before, she suddenly realized. It was always there. Pain. Sadness. Heartache. It called to her.

She lifted a hand to stroke the side of his jaw, a day's growth of beard prickly beneath her touch. She found his mouth, swiped the pad of her finger across his lower lip, his eyes changing, softening, heating. Such a good man. So many ghosts in the dark.

"Kiss me," she said softly.

His big hands cupped the back of her head, but his touch was gentle, his lips covering her own, and there it was again. Once upon a time she'd jumped on a horse's back without a saddle or a bridle. For a few glorious minutes she'd been as unfettered as a bird, the ground flying beneath them, arms outstretched, head tilted back. She felt the same way now.

Her mouth opened, and the touch of his tongue was as delicate as a feather. There was something about kissing this man, something that both frightened and enticed her at the same time. When his hand lowered, she arched because she wanted his touch. That, too, frightened her. She'd never felt such need. It was like the ache for food, a ravenous hunger that made her hands drop so she could unbutton his shirt. She went at it blind, preferred kissing him to drawing back and focusing on the task at hand because she didn't want to be parted from him. Ever. His gaze found hers, making her aware of where they were and what they were doing and how they shouldn't.

"Don't stop," he said.

And in his words she heard a plea for help, a desperate cry for her to save him from something.

What?

She searched his eyes, saw his desire for her, but also a longing that had nothing to do with sex, and it called to her because deep in her heart she knew. She felt the same need to be one with someone. All the years of going it alone, of wishing for a man's presence in her life even though she told herself she didn't need one, and she didn't…she really didn't, but that didn't take away the yearning for a man to look at her like Colby did right now.

She led him to his bed in the corner of the room. Her hands shook. Her heart ran in a marathon. Her mind ran circles.

What are you doing? Who cares? I need this. I shouldn't.

Round and round. And yet she started to unbutton his shirt once again. She used his eyes as anchors. They held her steady in a sea of uncertainty.

When his shirt slid off his shoulders something caught her gaze. His tattoo. A circle on his upper arm. No, a Celtic circle. But there was something odd about the lines. She shifted slightly, looked more closely.

Names.

They were the names of his men. Half a dozen of them swirling around an infinity loop. Her gaze shot to his, and she saw the sadness again, and the symbolism of the ink robbed her of breath, made her lean toward him and press her lips against his forearm, before moving closer and resting her cheek against his chest. She felt his arms slip around her. He held her tight, so tight she could barely breathe, but that was okay because he needed this.

He needed *her*.

There were a few things in this world she knew to be true. Her love for her daughter. Her daughter's love for her. Her family's love for both of them. And her growing love for this man. This damaged, wonderful, frightened man who loved animals and had the purest of souls and a sadness in his eyes that brought tears to her eyes.

Yes, he needed her. But she needed him, too.

Chapter 16

There had been moments in Colby's life when he'd been terrified out of his mind. This was one of them.

And yet…

Holding Jayden near the edge of his bed, pressing his cheek against the top of her head, inhaling her fragrance, quelled his fears, made his mind slow. He wanted to memorize the way it felt to have her in his arms, to be able to bring that memory back out at a later date and examine it and maybe use it as a reminder of how for one perfect moment everything had been right with the world.

She shifted and he thought, *This is it. This is when she realizes what a complete mess I am and walks out.*

She pulled her shirt off.

He stood there in shock, not just because she stared up at him half-naked, but at her steely-eyed look of resolve.

"Are you sure?" he asked.

She kicked off her boots in response, unsnapped her pants, shoved the denim down, straightened, her chin lifting, standing in front of him in nothing more than lace underwear and a matching bra.

And she was stunning.

She reached up, released her hair from its ponytail, her eyes a vivid blue, like the color of the deepest part of a flame. She took his breath away, and he wondered what he'd done to deserve such a perfect example of femininity.

Her hands moved to his jeans, the brush of her fingers causing his eyes to close. It'd been so long…

His jeans began to slide down, and he felt something hot brush up against his belly. Her breath. Sweet heaven above, she was killing him.

Something that sounded like a groan came from his throat. He opened his eyes, glanced down; she was on her knees, trying to lift his foot, something he hadn't even realized, he'd been so engrossed in the fantasy of her touching him with her mouth and using her tongue…

"Lift."

He gave her his foot. She tugged first one boot off, then the other, then slid his jeans down, leaving his boxers behind. And then she looked up at him, began to kiss his legs, first one, then the other.

He couldn't watch.

If he did he'd lose it right then and there, and suddenly he wanted this to be about her. He had to prove to her that there was one thing, at least, that he was good at. Or that he used to be good at.

And so he bent and helped her up, lifting her, moving her to the bed, and gently set her down, unable to do more than stare once she lay on the bed. Once, when he'd been younger, he and his dad traveled overseas to visit one of his dad's best customers, a Jordanian prince who'd had the most amazing collection of marble sculptures he'd ever seen. Jayden was like the living embodiment of those finely sculpted treasures. Her legs were long and perfectly formed, as if someone had drawn them first and then brought them to life. Her hips flared, her belly above the thin wisp of underwear flat until the point of her belly button, where it sank inward, begging for the touch of his hand or his mouth. She had the curves of a woman, a real woman, not one of those model-thin girls who never ate and used to chase him back when he was Colby Kotch, heir to a billion-dollar fortune. Her breasts were soft mounds, and he shook with a desire to touch them, or to lift the fabric of her bra and run his tongue around the pink nub.

"You're so beautiful."

His eyes met hers, and he saw them flare, and then her lashes lowered and she said, "Not anymore. Not after having a baby."

She was so off base that all he could do was stare at her, incredulous, until he slowly lowered himself next to her, resting on one side of her, his hand skating across the belly she thought so unattractive.

"You are the most incredible creature I've ever seen." His finger found the hollow that led to her belly button. She gasped. "And the fact that you've brought life into this world—" he bent and kissed her gently "—it makes you even more beautiful to me."

She still didn't look convinced, and so he kissed her again, trying to convince her with his mouth and then his touch that she turned him on in ways no one had ever done before.

Her lips opened beneath his, and he captured the tip of her tongue, sucking her and tasting her and thinking not even the ripest of cherries could be as sweet, as soft, as juicy as she was. Her lips were like the fuzz of a peach, and the way she moaned in response to his kiss, it jolted him like the shock of a bomb blast.

His hand dropped, sliding the edges of her panties down, his fingers dipping beneath them, his need to pleasure her as great as his need to protect her. That was what she did to him, made him feel like a man, like she was the most precious thing in the world and only he could keep her safe.

Her head turned, she gasped for breath, crying his name, and at first, all he did was tease her. His own body throbbed in response, but he wouldn't give in to the urge to cover her and do more. Instead he kissed her more deeply, mimicking his hand motions with his tongue, and she started to whimper.

Fly, he silently told her.

"No." She'd wrenched her mouth away. "I want you to enjoy this, too."

And then she made a move that would have done his hand-to-hand combat instructors proud: she rolled, capturing him beneath her, and he released a grunt of surprise and pleasure and frustration because he didn't want her to take control. He wanted to be the one to hold back, needed to do that, for her.

He flipped her beneath him. They ended up in the middle of his bed. Her eyes popped open and he saw laughter in them and it made him freeze for a moment because there was such joy in those eyes, her beauty so awe-inspiring all he could do was stare.

"No fair," she said.

But then he pushed against her, and her eyes closed and she groaned and thrust her head back, and he knew he'd won. He captured her lips again, but this time it was no gentle seduction. This time it was all about making her moan and cry out in pleasure as he moved his body up and down, her legs wrapping around him, and it was hell—Lord, how it was hell—to hold back when all he wanted to do was rip the flimsy strip of fabric away and drop his boxers and take her. But he couldn't do that. He didn't have protection.

She wrenched her head, left, right, and he reared back and watched her hair splay around her, sweat glistening on her brow, her cheeks flushing, the pulse at her throat throbbing.

"Oh, Colby!"

And still he maintained control, his mouth finding the beat at the base of her neck, his teeth nipping her flesh, his hips moving back and forth. She became more frenetic beneath him and he knew she was about to lose control, and it gave him such purpose, such happiness to know that he'd succeeded.

He sensed the moment it happened. She froze, but only for a split second, and then she fell back against the bed, and he watched as her pleasure at long last took flight, her lips parting, tears sliding from the corner of her eyes as she cried out his name. He watched, aching in a way he'd never ached before, a physical pain that came from ignoring his own needs in favor of her own, but he wouldn't have changed a thing, not for all the money in the world. This…holding her, bringing her pleasure, it made his heart sing in a way he'd never felt before.

And happiness was not something he'd ever thought to feel again.

* * *

His weight should have crushed her. That was Jayden's first thought as reality returned and his room came into sharp focus. How long had he been holding her? One minute? Two? Five?

"Do you need me to move?" he whispered.

Yes. She needed him to roll on his back so she could do to him what he'd done to her. That was what she wanted. He'd turned her into a wanton. Into the woman she'd been back before she'd become a mother when all she'd wanted to do was feel the intense pleasure of being with a man. And, damn, she still shook from the force of what he'd done to her.

"Roll onto your back."

He didn't move. She pushed on his chest. All he did was tip sideways, his right leg covering her own, his hand landing on her belly.

"We don't have protection." His eyes studied her, roving over her face, a slight smile tipping the edges of his lips. "It's fine."

No, it wasn't fine. "This isn't just about me."

"Why not?"

"Because."

She pressed back into the soft comfort of his bed. His hair was tousled, his skin tanned compared to her own. For the first time she realized how much bigger he was than her, from the width of his shoulders to the breadth of his chest. Whorls of hair sprouted from the hard surface of his pecs. She found herself lifting a hand and circling the hardened contours of them. His muscles contracted.

"You should get dressed." His smile turned tender. "I'd hate for someone to wonder where we both are."

Get dressed? Who was he kidding?

"I don't have to go anywhere right away."

His face was a study of contrasts. In his eyes she saw desire mixed with caution. Joy mixed with the ever-present sadness. Pride mixed with humility. She couldn't stop herself from touching that face, from running her fingers down the side of his hardened jaw, marveling at the color of his eyes.

"Why are you fighting this?"

She hadn't meant to ask the question, but it'd been hovering there, the truth they sought to avoid clinging to the side of a cliff, both of them not at all ready for the fall.

He stared down at her, and she knew he recognized her need for truth. "We don't have protection," he repeated.

"Actually, I'm on birth control." She swiped a lock of his hair off his face. "And don't tell me you don't have something in this room of yours, too."

His pupils contracted, and she went still for a moment because she could tell he was carefully considering his words. He looked frightened all of a sudden. And sad. And it finally hit her what was going on.

"Is this your penance, Colby? Part of how you punish yourself for what happened in the past?"

He didn't move. Didn't say anything. She could tell he tried to process if what she said was true.

Her fingers tightened around the edge of the blanket. "Don't hold back, Colby. Let yourself go."

"You're way off base."

"Am I?" She studied his face for clues that she was wrong. "You didn't die on the battlefield, so you killed yourself off in another way."

"That's enough."

She reached for her clothes, knowing he was angry, but she didn't care. She pulled on her jeans, and she didn't feel anger or disappointment in return, just a deep disappointment in herself. For years she'd held herself back from men, had prided herself on her control and her commitment to focusing on her future, and then the first attractive man had come along, boom, back into old habits.

Her hands shook as she buttoned her jeans. Tears blurred her vision. What an idiot.

He hadn't even moved. She supposed that was best.

"Goodbye, Colby."

Chapter 17

She had it all wrong.

The words had followed him to bed that night, a ghost that haunted his dreams and robbed him of sleep, although his insomnia might also have had something to do with his conversation with Bryan. Nightmares. He hadn't had one in a long, long time, had thought them banished from his mind, but the visceral images had risen to the surface with only a mention of his past.

Doesn't mean anything.

The bigger issue was what the hell to do now. In a half hour she'd arrive for work, and that meant acting as if nothing had happened. Worse, today was a day when he wouldn't be able to avoid her. They were taking a group of guests out on horseback to a nearby lake. That would entail working side by side with her, and now, after what had happened last night, he didn't know how the hell he'd focus on work.

He tossed his breakfast dishes into the sink, the things clattering a little too hard, so much so that he almost didn't hear his cell phone chime. Crazy thing was, his heart punched his rib cage, and that was how much he wanted it to be Jayden. It wasn't. It was Jax.

Mind a quick meeting?

He stared at the words in the comment bubble. It wasn't uncommon for Jax to make such a request. His boss kept a close eye on things. What was uncommon was the time. Usually they met after the day was over, usually over a beer, more often than not in his boss's backyard while they went over the business side of Hooves for Heroes.

Sure. Where?

I'm in your office.

Colby didn't waste any time, the beat of his heart chasing him the whole way down the hall. In all his years working for the man, he'd never requested an early-morning meeting. Popping in to say hello, yes. Meeting? No.

"Good morning." Jax stood with his back to the window that overlooked their back pasture, hands tucked into his jeans pockets, his black polo shirt with *Hooves for Heroes* silk-screened on the left breast matching Colby's own shirt. It was still early, the mountains in the distance shielding the sun from the valley below and casting the land in browns and grays and dirty greens. "Thanks for coming in early."

"I was already on my way." He tried to smile, wasn't very successful at it, ended up crossing his arms in front of him and perching on the corner of his desk. For some reason he felt about as tense as a mouse with a hawk flying overhead.

"Big day today. Taking some of the crew out to the lake."

Jax nodded. "That ought to be fun. Looks like it'll be a nice day for it. Probably a little easier for you two now that Derrick is back."

"It is," he said. "I can't wait to get out there."

"I heard you had a breakthrough with Bryan."

So that was what this was about? Relief lowered Colby's shoulders. It made it easier to look the man in his eyes, too. He debated whether to sit down behind his desk or not, but he always felt awkward when his boss stood while he sat.

"We did, but it was Jayden who instigated the whole thing."

Jax nodded. "Bryan mentioned she turned him loose in the arena."

"Yup. But once he started riding around he quit complaining, and then I think we could all tell he liked it. He'd never admit it, but his silence was admission enough."

"Well, I'm glad you stuck with it," Jax said.

"Me, too."

His boss had a habit of lapsing into silence, and of taking his time to form his words, especially when he had something important to say. So when the room went quiet again, Colby knew he had it all wrong. This wasn't about Bryan. This was about something else entirely.

"Look, Colby, it goes without saying that we love

you. You're a member of our family, so please don't take what I'm about to say in the wrong way."

His boss lapsed into silence again. When Jax took a deep breath, it reminded Colby of the doctors he used to deal with. They'd take a deep breath before delivering bad news.

"Derrick saw Jayden leaving your apartment last evening."

Colby felt his muscles go rigid.

"I don't want you to think I disapprove." For the first time since Colby had met Jaxton Stone, he sounded uncertain of himself. "Well, on a professional level, I do. These days employers have to be so careful when it comes to interoffice affairs—"

His head snapped up. "It's not an affair."

Jax went back to studying him again. "It's not?"

"It's over." He steadied himself by clutching the desk he leaned against. "We talked about it last night…after." God help him, he'd never been more mortified in his life.

One of Jax's brows lifted, but then it dropped and he said, "Look. You're family to us, Colby. I hope you know that. And Naomi and I have really grown fond of Jayden. You guys are both good people. I just came down here to say if there's something going on between you, if you're secretly dating or something, that's okay. We understand. These things happen. I just think we should dot our i's and cross our t's is all. Have a sit-down with the both of you. Maybe sign something. It'd be for your protection as well as Hooves for Heroes."

Colby's fingers had begun to ache. "We don't need to do that."

"No?" The brow lifted again.

"It won't happen again."

Jax scuffed the back of his hair with a hand, and for the first time he looked as uncomfortable as Colby felt. "Look, I'm going to go out on a limb and say something I probably shouldn't, and I hope you don't mind. The thing is, Naomi and I, we've both watched you over the past few years, and we've both noticed how you never go out or do anything fun, and we both think that, I don't know, maybe dating Jayden might be good for you, *not*—" he held up his hands "—that we want you to chase after her or anything like that." He ran his hands through his hair again. "Damn, I'm making a mess of this. Bottom line. You've got one life to live and you're not living yours. It's not good for you, Colby. Naomi and I both feel that way. Maybe, I don't know, it might be good for you to sit down with one of our counselors, talk it out."

What a perfect start to his day. His boss telling him he needed therapy.

"Point taken."

Jax wore his relief like a prisoner just pardoned from jail. "Okay, great. Again, great work with Bryan. Keep up the good work. I'll catch up with you later this week."

But when his boss left the office, Colby clutched his head with both hands.

Damn it.

One thing was clear. This thing with Jayden had to end. He needed to stop thinking about her, too. Needed to banish her from his mind.

He just wished he knew how.

It had not been a good night. Jayden sat in front of the barn for a full five minutes trying to gain some form of composure. It didn't help.

She'd spent the whole damn night alternating between complete embarrassment and utter despair. As a woman who prided herself on control, she'd blown it. Her first job post college what did she do?

The tears threatened to fall again.

She'd developed feelings for a man who clearly didn't want to be loved…or to love her back.

Dumb, dumb, dumb.

So, okay. She was a big girl. She'd made a mistake, had developed feelings for someone she shouldn't have, and his rejection of her was probably for the best. She'd worked too long and too hard to risk turning her life upside down on a chance she could repair a broken man.

Her insides twisted as she got out of the car, the early-morning air so chilly it made her cheeks feel almost wet. They would start later today than normal. They had half a dozen horses to saddle up for today's trail ride to the lake. They'd be packing in other equipment, too. Fishing poles, food, water. At least they wouldn't have to deal with Bryan. He'd opted out of today's adventure, as had a few of their other guests. Initially, when she'd been told about the outing, she'd been thrilled. Now all she felt was dread. Colby didn't help matters.

"You and Derrick get started on saddling the horses. We'll use Beau to pack in supplies. I'll get him ready. Leave the halters on the horses. We'll need to tie them later."

That was his greeting to her. Not that she'd expected more. What she hadn't expected was the shock to her system his voice provided. The sexy male baritone that had driven her to the edge of reason last night. But it wasn't just a physical reaction that nearly brought her to her knees. It was the emotional jolt to her system, the memory of what it was like to hold him and to rest her head against his chest and to have thought, for however brief a moment, that maybe things would work out between them. She'd been wrong. Dead wrong. And the realization that she'd never have that again was akin to the loss she'd felt when her mom had died. Different, yes, but so achingly similar.

"Why don't Derrick and I start at opposite ends. We can work our way toward the middle."

There. He wasn't the only one who could pretend that everything was all right.

"That will work. I'll grab the saddles and bridles and bring them to you two."

He pulled his gaze away, and Jayden stood in the middle of the aisle, the cold from the ground seeping into her bones. She might have been a fool to let things get so out of hand. She might have jeopardized a job she loved and a heart that'd already been broken. But she was damn good at her job.

It didn't take long to saddle six horses. She was glad for the work. It helped to soothe her nerves.

"Anything else I can help you with?" Derrick asked, his smile the first one she'd seen that day.

"We might need help getting everyone up on horseback," Colby said.

The man's gray eyes studied them both and she wondered if he sensed the tension in the air. "No problem."

Voices reached them, and she knew their wounded warriors made their way toward the arena. Some, like Dylan, bore noticeable battle scars. Others, like their one female guest, carried everything inside. Marjorie reminded Jayden of a bird she'd found outside her parents' home that had been terrified of her surroundings but in desperate need of help. Marjorie was one of their first responders, a cop who'd been wounded by some guy hopped up on drugs. The encounter had left more than physical scars behind.

"Are you guys ready?" Colby asked them.

"All right, people. We're going to start mounting you up one at a time." Colby's words rang through the barn. "Who wants to go first?"

She heard the *clip-clop* of horse's hooves a moment later as Derrick led Zippy out of a stall. She went and fetched Annie. That appeared to be the right thing to do, because Colby nodded ever so slightly. They all met up out front, and in less than two minutes someone else was in the saddle, Marjorie this time, the dark-haired woman barely smiling as she looked down at her.

They repeated the process until all nine riders were mounted. She'd picked Dover for her own mount. Beau, the horse they would use for packing in the supplies, was being led by Colby.

"I'll hold down the fort," Derrick said. "Get to work on that broken pipe out back."

"Sounds good," Colby said, his gaze meeting hers. "You take the back. I'll take the front," Colby ordered. He didn't wait for a reply, just kicked his horse into a trot, Beau doing the same, then rode up ahead of everyone, waving his arm when he got there. "Everyone follow me."

Dylan pulled up alongside her. "Can I ride with you?"

She nodded without thinking about it. Dover didn't need any urging. She knew the drill, following into line behind the other horses.

"You seem a little down and out." Dylan's face was such a contrast from Colby's stony-faced countenance that her heart hurt thinking about it. "You okay?"

Why couldn't she have found the man attractive or returned his smile? Well, aside from the obvious problem of him being a guest, but after he was gone, how much easier would it have been to return the interest of a man who didn't bear the weight of the world on his shoulders, or who refused to let go of his past.

"Just busy," she replied. "We have a lot of guests to keep an eye on today."

"No need to worry about me. I've taken to this riding thing like a duck to water."

He had. And he genuinely seemed to enjoy it. And he was handsome and kind, and yet she looked at Dylan and felt...nothing.

"It's the ducks that can't swim that I worry about." She waved, kicking Dover forward and calling out, "Marjorie, just pull back on the reins a little. She'll slow down."

Dylan seemed to take the hint, falling back into line with the others as they rode toward the lake, which Colby had told her sat on land belonging to their neighbor. The Reynolds family had granted Hooves for Heroes access, but it would take them a little over an hour to get there. It would go fast, though, Jayden could already tell.

"Wow," she heard someone say when they crested a small rise, and she'd been so busy moving back and forth between guests she hadn't even realized they'd arrived.

It was Dylan who'd spoken, and she would have to agree. A body of water came into view, one so big the sky was reflected in its surface, puffy clouds seeming to dot the water, Jayden thinking whimsically that it looked like they could jump from cloud to cloud. A home sat at the far end, but it seemed tiny from their vantage point, like a dollhouse in a make-believe world.

"This place is amazing," Marjorie whispered.

"Just what the doctor ordered," Dylan echoed.

They rode nose to tail down a narrow path that led to the lake's edge and a large oak tree with a rope swing beneath it. Someone had lugged a few picnic tables to the area, although for the life of her she couldn't figure out how. There were no roads, nothing but rolling hills and serene valleys and oak trees as far as the eye could see. Must have been a heck of a truck ride to transport the things to the middle of nowhere.

"We'll tie the horses to a rope line." Colby had pulled up in front of them all. "Hang on while I get everything sorted out."

"You need help?" she asked as he dismounted.

He didn't answer. She hopped off her horse. Sooner or later they'd have to get used to working together despite what had happened between them.

"I can do it," he snapped.

His words had the same effect as the crack of a whip. She actually took a step back. She saw him stiffen, saw him clasp the sides of his saddle, saw his big shoulders rise and fall and knew that he tried to gain control. Her heart softened then because she knew how he struggled. So many demons from his past. She had them, too, but hers were nothing compared to his.

"Thanks anyway," he said.

She stared at his rigid back, watched as he went about the task of stringing a rope between two trees; all the while her heart pounded in her chest. She didn't want to see him upset, but there was nothing she could do, and the feeling of helplessness made her eyes burn.

They'd played with fire…and they'd both ended up burned.

Chapter 18

He'd never felt more trapped in his life.

The bark of the tree he leaned against bit into his back, but Colby hardly noticed. He watched from a distance as their wounded veterans fished or swam or, in Marjorie's case, read. Jayden sat on a picnic table talking to Dylan. The man hadn't left her side. And see, that was the thing. It shouldn't have made him feel eaten up by jealousy, but it did.

She must have felt his stare, because she glanced over at him, her dark hair flicking over a shoulder, and he tensed because she said something to Dylan and he knew what she was about to do.

No, don't. Stay there. Stay away.

She waved, slid off the tabletop she'd been sitting on and headed in his direction.

Damn.

"Hey," she said softly.

This wasn't how he'd predicted she'd behave. He'd thought after last night she'd be mad at him. He'd assumed she'd keep her distance. He should have known better. Nothing was ever easy where Jayden was concerned. He remembered having that very thought the day he'd first met her. Little did he know where things would end up.

"We'll be leaving in a half hour." He tried to keep his voice even, tried not to let her hear just how much her presence affected him. "You might want to tell everyone so they can start getting ready."

Her face was dappled by sunlight, her eyes as blue as the surface of the lake behind her, and he committed the image to memory, because she just seemed to grow more beautiful with each passing day. Her cheeks were flushed and matched the rose color of her lips. If he closed his eyes he could perfectly recall how those lips had felt against his own, and how she'd tasted like cherry, so sweet. The memory had haunted him all night.

"I don't want things to be awkward between us," she said.

He almost laughed. Awkward? That was what she called this? Forgetting someone's name was awkward. This was hell.

"If you want, you can get started checking the horses' tack. I'll start rounding everyone up." He took a step toward the lake, the need to leave overwhelming him.

She caught him with her hand. She made him feel like the earth was tilting sideways, and Colby desperately tried to hang on to something, anything, but not her hand. That he couldn't do. He tried to pull away. She wouldn't let him.

"I can't be angry with you anymore." In her eyes he saw a sadness as deep as the ocean. "Last night I was frustrated. Hurt that you wouldn't open up to me. I know what you went through was terrible, and I'm sorry I brought it up."

He wanted to jerk away, or to yell at the top of his lungs, maybe jump on the back of a horse and ride until the wind caught his tears and his mind went numb.

"You were right, though." He'd wanted her to stay away, had used the tension between them as a barrier, but he didn't like it, either, he admitted. In that moment he realized Jayden had become his friend. He'd missed her companionship today.

She dropped his hand. He inhaled like a man atop the highest of peaks, as if oxygen was scarce and it was all he could do to gasp in enough air to survive.

"I'm messed up, Jayden." He hated the way her eyes grew big and the way her lips began to tremble. "I tried to open up to you. I really did. That night. In my room. I wanted to let go, but I just…couldn't."

"It's okay." She reached for his hand again. He stepped back, and he saw pain flow into her eyes. "I realize that now, Colby. I'm sorry I got upset."

"Don't apologize." He could take anything but that.

"I stormed out and I shouldn't have."

"And I should have never let things get so out of hand."

Her chin tipped up. "It takes two to tango."

"And two people who care for each other to make things work."

It was her turn to draw back. "What do you mean?"

"I can't do it, Jayden. Last night I was thinking I could

let it all go, that I could take that next step, but I can't. My feelings for you just aren't that deep."

Lies.

Because he loved her; the realization hit him with the force of a baseball bat. That was why he stood in front of her now, why he held still as he watched her eyes fill with tears and why it hurt him to hear the sigh of pain she released. He loved her, but he couldn't be with her because he would hurt her in the end.

"There's chemistry between us. That I won't deny. But more than that? Nah." He shook his head. "There's nothing there. That's why I stopped. My job's too important to risk a quick fling."

She searched his eyes. "You're lying."

It took every ounce of his strength to keep the truth out of his eyes. He loved her so much that he would sacrifice his own happiness for her own.

"I'm just trying to keep it real," he said.

He saw her tip her chin up, saw the faint stain of anger color her cheeks. He'd hurt her and now she was angry and he didn't blame her.

"I'll go tell the guests we're getting ready to leave," he said.

Because he needed to escape, had to step away from her before he did something completely unconscionable, like pull her into his arms and tell her everything would be okay. With him, nothing would be okay. History had proved that fact.

"Are you sure?"

Jax Stone stared at her from across the expanse of his desk, concern in his eyes. His dog Tramp lifted his head, peering at the two humans as if sensing the tension between them, too.

"I don't really feel as if I have a choice," Jayden admitted, trying hard not to let her emotions get the better of her. "I didn't mean for it to happen. I really didn't. But it will be too hard to work with him now that it has."

He studied her in that quiet way of his. "Would it help to tell you that I already knew about you and Colby?"

His words were like being jabbed with a stick. "What?"

"Derrick saw you leaving his room. I talked to Colby about it this morning. He reassured me there was nothing between you two."

"There isn't. Well, there is, or there was, but I suppose it doesn't matter. I don't think I can work with him now." She sounded hoarse even to her own ears. "I have a friend from school, someone who grew up on a ranch. Her name's Chandra, and she'd be perfect for my job. And I'd train her so it wouldn't feel as if you were starting over from scratch. It shouldn't take me long. I picked up on things pretty quickly here, so maybe I wouldn't have to work the entire two weeks."

She stared at the piece of paper she'd slid across the desk earlier. Her hastily scribbled notice of resignation. It was like a white beacon on his desk. A caution sign for what could go wrong in your life if you let your foolish fantasies get in the way of reality.

"Forgive me if this seems like prying," Jax said softly. "But do you have feelings for him? *Deep* feelings?"

She tipped her chin up, wanting her boss to know that she held him no ill will. "No." *Deep breath. You can hold it together.* "Well, maybe a little."

He shook his head. "Then let me give this back to you." He slid the paper in her direction. "I told Colby we could work this out. If you have feelings for each other, I'd be the last person in the world to get in the way of that. My own wife worked for me before we married."

"He doesn't have feelings for me. That's the problem."

Her voice sounded strangled, and she realized it was because tears hung on the edge of her lashes. She was about to completely lose it in front of her boss.

"So you feel the best way to handle the matter is to leave?"

Why did it sound so cowardly when he put it that way?

"I just think it's the smart thing to do." Because being near Colby was too hard. Somehow, she'd lost control of her life, and she needed to get it back.

She *had* to get it back.

This was exactly the type of situation her dad had predicted would happen to her. She refused to live up to his expectations. Or maybe down.

So her hands clenched in her lap. Jax studied her in the same way a cop would probably study a teenager who'd just been pulled over for speeding. She tried not to grow uncomfortable under that stare.

"I guess there's not much to say, then." He made a steeple with his hands, the light from the window to her right catching the strands of his hair and making them look more gray than they really were. "Aside from the fact that we will miss you and that I really wish I could change your mind."

Her breaths came faster and faster as she fought to hold it together. "Thank you." Her fingernails dug into her jeans. "I've really enjoyed working here."

"But do you mind if I make a suggestion?"

She froze.

"I think we should hold off on telling Colby. At least for a few days while I vet that friend of yours. Plus, it gives you a day or two to think things over."

"That would be fine." She wasn't going to change her mind. But waiting to tell Colby gave her a few days to steel her resolve against the inevitable objections Colby would raise. It would be just like him to volunteer to leave instead of her, and she didn't want that. Colby was as much a part of this ranch as her boss and his family and all the horses and everything she'd come to admire over the past few weeks.

"Jayden, I hope you don't mind me saying, but I think you're making a mistake."

Her legs had started to shake. It took a few deep breaths to inject some willpower into her spine, but the kindness in his eyes nearly undid the lead line on her control.

"I'm not going to pretend that I have any right to weigh in on your life choices. In fact, I'm probably breaking some kind of employer code of ethics by saying this, but I think you and Colby should try to work things out. I don't know what happened. It's none of my business, but I think of Colby like a younger brother. And I look at you and I can't help but think how perfect you two are for each other. I know he's got some baggage, but if I'm not mistaken, I think you have some, too. I think that's why you're quitting. You're afraid of making the same mistake twice. Take it from me. Don't make big life decisions based on fear."

How did he know that?

She stood sharply, had to because if she didn't, she'd start bawling. She wouldn't do that. It'd be the final humiliation. Darn it all. Even her boss's dog seemed to stare up at her in concern.

"Thank you for everything, Jax. And if you don't mind, can you let me know before you tell Colby? I'm sure he'll have some choice words for me, and I'd like time to prepare."

"He won't." Jax stood, too. "I'll make sure he respects your decision, and that will include keeping his opinions to himself."

"Thank you," she said through a throat gone thick with unshed tears. She couldn't get to the office door fast enough.

"Jayden."

She couldn't turn and face him, though. As if tethered by the chair she'd sat in, her tears had started to fall.

"Promise me you'll think about what I said."

She nodded. But there was nothing to say. Not really. She'd made her bed, so to speak; now she had to lie in it.

But as she walked to her car she vowed she would never, ever lose control of her emotions again.

Chapter 19

It was hell.

Colby's hand clenched the saddle he removed from Zippy's back, the big sorrel turning his head to look at him as if silently asking, "What's wrong?"

What was wrong?

His whole damn life. Jayden had been nothing but kind over the past forty-eight hours. Impersonal, but kind. She could barely look at him, and who could blame her? He'd cut her off at the knees, and not for the reason she thought. He'd done it out of self-preservation.

Coward.

It'd taken him exactly twenty-four hours after they'd gotten back from the trail ride to realize she was right. He hadn't denied his feelings for her out of some kind of misplaced professionalism, but because he was scared. Bone-deep, gut-twisting, falling-off-a-cliff scared.

"If that's all for the day, I think I'm going to go." Her voice was soft, courteous, professional. "Derrick said he'd help you feed once he was done mucking."

Her voice came from his left; the saddle was hanging like dead weight in his arms, his inability to face her one of the many cowardly traits he'd come down with this week.

"Great. Thanks for all your hard work." He'd used the same impersonal tone. Derrick was around somewhere and he knew he might be listening to every word.

He had no idea if she nodded or smiled or even waved goodbye. All he heard was the retreat of her booted feet down the barn aisle. He hefted the saddle again, resting the pommel on his hips so he'd have a free hand to grab the bridle that hung on a peg to his left.

He nearly dropped it when he ducked under the cross ties.

"Son of—"

"You okay?" Derrick called from inside one of the stalls.

"Fine, fine."

Her car started out front, and then it kicked up gravel as she put the vehicle in Reverse. But she didn't drive off in a hurry. That was the way she'd been all week. Careful. Measured. Distant.

And it made his stomach roll. Yeah. He cared for her. Cared for her too much.

Zippy's food was already in his feeder thanks to Jayden's hard work. He'd closed the stall door when he heard a vehicle arrive. Whoever it was, he'd find out soon enough. Colby continued going through and spot-checking all the horses in his care. They were all bedded down in ankle-deep shavings. More of Jayden's handiwork.

A door slammed.

Probably Jax. His boss had said he'd wanted to talk to him about something. Had asked him to stop by later. Back to their regularly scheduled programming of meeting in the evenings. He turned toward the opening at the end of the barn aisle.

And froze.

It was as if every speck of air had been sucked from the building. As if day had suddenly turned to night, and his world had been tipped end over end.

"Hello, son."

It had been five years since he'd last seen the man. Five years since Liz had come to him, crying, confessing her sins, and then committing an even greater transgression by admitting she'd fallen in love with his dad. The sight of him standing there shot emotions through Colby he hadn't even known he'd had.

His rage culminated in two words. "Get out."

"Colby, please."

How the hell had he found him? Jax? He didn't think his boss would betray him. It wasn't his style, which meant his dad had tracked him down, and he supposed that shouldn't be a surprise. He had more money than God.

"You look good, son."

"I *said*, get out." He kept his words low, mindful of Derrick's presence.

His dad took another step closer. Colby held out a hand. "Stop."

"Would it surprise you to know I've been checking up on you for years?"

No, that didn't surprise him. Deep inside, in those rare moments when he allowed himself to think about the man he'd once loved, he'd wondered if his dad would do that.

"I don't care what you've been doing with your time, least of all now that I've settled into my own life, away from you. You're dead to me. I told you that on the day you and Liz admitted what'd been going on."

His dad came forward despite his protestations. Age had not been kind to him, Colby realized. A face that had once been so much like his own had been grooved by the hand of time, or maybe the guilt of living with what he'd done to his only son. Colby didn't know, didn't care. His hair was completely gray now. And the man who'd once stood so tall seemed shorter somehow. Or maybe that was Colby's perception of the man who'd once seemed larger than life, but who'd been reduced to someone petty and small.

"Liz is no longer in my life."

"So I heard. Too bad. You two were perfect for each other."

His dad took yet another step. He still dressed the same. Tailored pants, off-white polo shirt. Custom loafers. Same gold watch. Same blue eyes. Colby had always wondered what he would do if he came face-to-face with the man. He admitted then he didn't care enough to feel anything but rage.

"I deserve that." He stuffed his hands in his pockets. "There's nothing I can say to defend my actions other than I had a lot on my plate back then."

"Oh, spare me the sob story, Dad." The coals of his fury flared to life. "I'd just been medically discharged. I could barely walk. I'd been in the worse firefight of my life. And I was reeling from the pain of losing men I loved like brothers. I'd thought I could recover in the one place in the world where I felt safe, and what did you and Liz do?"

The veins in his dad's eyes had begun to redden, and Colby stared at him in shock. The only time he'd seen the man cry was when Colby's mom died.

"I'm sorry, son. I came here to say that to you. Finally. That's all. I'm sorry. I regret what happened more than you could know."

The words had come out sounding thick with tears. Crocodile tears? Colby didn't know, still didn't care. The wound his father had inflicted on him was still too deep. Unforgivable, really.

"Please leave."

His dad took one more step. They were only a few feet away from each other now, close enough that Colby could see the tiny lines around his lips. The hollows beneath his eyes. The ravages of a guilty conscience. Well, good. Served him right. His dad had always prided himself on looking younger than his years. Not anymore.

"I'd like you to move back to Texas."

Of all the...

"You just don't get it, do you?" Colby snapped. "I told you years ago, I'm done with that life. Done with you. Done with it all."

He swung around, heading God knew where because he just wanted to get away from the man who'd broken his heart all those years ago.

"Son." His dad swung him around. Colby balled his fist. But the tears in his dad's eyes stopped him. It hit him then. The man he had once loved and so admired was a broken man. All the wealth in the world hadn't made him happy. It was a lesson Colby had learned overseas. The true joys in life came from the people you surrounded yourself with, not money. Never money.

And then he'd let his buddies die.

He took a step back, sucked in a breath. This wasn't about him. This was about the man who called himself a father and was anything but.

"I feel sorry for you, Dad." And he did. He'd come all the way to California to make his amends. Only now did his dad realize some things just couldn't be forgiven. "Go back to Texas. I'm happy where I'm at."

Was he, though? The question seemed whispered like the sigh of the wind, blowing around, swiping at the cobwebs in his mind. Was he truly happy?

"Colby, please."

He kept walking, his mind reeling from it all. But then he stopped, slowly turned.

"I don't hate you, Dad. I just don't care."

Because it was impossible for him to care. He swung away again because he didn't want his dad to see his face crumple. He'd tucked away his heart, put it in a place where even someone like Jayden couldn't reach it.

"I'll leave my number with your boss."

"I already have it." He paused at the base of the stairs that led to his office and apartment. "For what it's worth, I accept your apology."

His dad's face crumpled. Even from the distance he was at, Colby saw it happen. Something inside Colby reacted to the sight, something he'd thought long dead; it had him clutching the rail and holding on for dear life.

He still loved his dad. Despite everything that had happened, he still had feelings for the man.

Unbelievable.

"Can I call you?" his dad asked.

"I don't know if I'll be here."

"What do you mean?"

He didn't know what he meant. He didn't know anything except he needed the sanctity of his apartment, a place where he could think.

"Son?"

A place where he could figure out just where the hell he'd gone so wrong.

"Goodbye, Dad."

Chapter 20

"What do you mean he's gone?"

Jayden stood in the middle of the barn aisle, the look on her boss's face one she'd never seen before.

"He just took off." Jax lifted the cowboy hat he wore, raking his fingers through his salt-and-pepper hair. "Came over to the house last night and told me he had something to do. Said you and Derrick would be fine on your own today, because we're transitioning out our first batch of veterans so we can bring in the new ones next week. I didn't have the heart to tell him no. The man's been here nearly five years and never taken a vacation. But I have to be honest, Jayden. I'm a little worried he won't be back. Naomi said he seemed shell-shocked."

"Did you tell him I'd quit?"

Jax shook his head. "Didn't have time. Derrick said he had a visitor last night." She watched her boss suck in a deep breath, his eyes full of concern. "His dad."

His… *"What?"*

"I know. Showed up out of the blue. Called me on my cell phone, although I have no idea how he got my number because I'm pretty much off the grid. Going to have to look into that, but the point is I think something his dad said has him spooked. Derrick said he couldn't hear much of what was said, but what he did hear sounded pretty heated. I checked the surveillance feeds and they didn't leave together, so I don't think he went back to Texas. I think this was something else."

Gone. She should have felt relief. Instead all she felt was an overwhelming sense of concern. He'd seen his father. Well, she knew firsthand how upsetting that could be. Colby might have wounded her to the core with his inability to care for her, but she didn't wish him ill, and she knew how much his father and that woman had hurt him.

"Look," Jax said. "If you want to call that friend of yours now, see if she's available to start today, that'd be great. I think it might be smart to start bringing her up to speed. Between you and Derrick, I think we'll be okay."

"I can do that."

"Great. I knew I could count on you."

She didn't have time to do much more than run around after that. Every once in a while she'd turn to look for Colby, to ask him a question, but he wasn't there. Soon enough her friend Chandra arrived. And that brought on a new batch of feelings, because once she brought Chandra up to speed, she'd be leaving, too, and she wondered if she'd even get to say goodbye to Colby.

Who cares if you don't get to say goodbye?

That was what she told herself, except there was no

sense in denying it anymore. He might have rejected her and it might have made her feel as if he'd taken her heart and tossed it on the ground and then used his toe to grind it into the dirt, but she still cared for him. She tried not to think about it. When she went home that night, she wrapped her arms around her daughter, holding her tight. And the next day, when Colby still wasn't back, she worked with Chandra. It helped to keep busy because every time she cracked the door on her feelings, her stomach tightened, and she had to turn away from examining the emotions she fought to keep contained.

He'd left...and he hadn't even said goodbye.

He drove all night.

He had no idea why it was so important for him to get to where he was going, just knew he had to get there before...

Before what?

Never once had he felt the urge to visit the grave of one of his fallen team members. And why Victor? Sure, he'd hit it off with the soft-spoken man who'd been raised in the same state he'd been. Victor had been younger than him by a couple of years, and if Colby were honest with himself, he'd tried to be a mentor to the young man.

And he'd been killed. On his watch.

The pain the words wrought had him blinking against tears. They surprised him. He'd been so good at keeping it in, the pain, the sadness, the disappointment in himself. And then his dad had visited, and it'd brought it all back.

He slept in his car when he got too sleepy to drive. Headed right back out and to the small town outside of

Dallas where he knew Victor was buried. The last time he'd been there had been for the funeral, when he'd handed the flag to Victor's mom, the young man's fiancée sitting next to her.

He'd never seen anyone look as heartbroken and shattered as Victor's fiancée. It still hurt to think about it.

He pulled into the cemetery and headed toward the American flag in the middle, the place where locals buried their military. The place where he'd stood years ago and watched as they'd lowered Victor's casket into the ground.

It took him a moment to get up the strength to leave his truck.

When you getting married? Colby had asked.

Soon as I get back, Victor had answered.

Colby's hands were clenched tight around the steering wheel. Finally he gathered his courage and slipped out of the truck, drawn to Victor's grave by a force he didn't understand. Bad idea? Good idea? He didn't know.

It took him a moment to find the grave. Didn't realize he was crying until he spotted Victor's name and the words were blurred. He wiped at his eyes.

"Damn, kid, it's been a while, huh?"

He closed his eyes, clenched his hands. He didn't know what to say. Didn't know why he'd driven so far to visit the grave of a fallen soldier.

Except…maybe he did know.

"I'm sorry," he told the young man. "I did everything I could to get you and the others out there. I really did."

He wiped at his eyes, his knees giving out, Colby kneeling on the grass in front of the alabaster grave marker.

"It should have been me," he said. "I was the one who

got us into trouble, not you. I should have never moved the team to that location. I should have just waited. But I didn't and now…"

He shook his head, wiped at his eyes again.

"It should have been me."

Except then he wouldn't have met Jayden. If none of it had happened he would have gone home to Texas, married Liz, maybe had a kid or two, but it wouldn't have been the same. What he felt for Jayden was so different and so much deeper than anything he'd ever felt before. The only thing that came close was how he'd felt toward his team.

"I think I understand why I was left behind now, though," he told Victor. "She needs me." He couldn't speak for a moment. "And I need her."

"You look like someone chewed you up and spat you back out."

It was Friday, and Bryan Vance was their last guest to leave before new ones would start to arrive next week. Their most troublesome wounded veteran rolled toward her, something that wasn't quite a smile, but wasn't exactly a frown, either, on his face. He'd been a model guest ever since that day when she'd forced him to ride on his own.

"Hard to say goodbye," she admitted. And not just to Bryan, but the other guests, too.

"Aww, come on. You won't miss me."

The man stared up at her with his serious brown eyes and she suddenly felt like crying. Why, she had no idea.

"Actually, I will miss you." She did something impulsive then, bent down and hugged him, the man stiff at first but then slowly relaxing. When she drew back, she would swear his eyes were rimmed with red.

"Thanks for everything, kid."

She reached for his scarred hand, squeezed it. "You're welcome."

They heard a vehicle approach and Jayden's heart jumped in her chest, but it was just the transport van coming for Bryan.

"You won't be missing me for long," the man said. "Jax invited me back. Said I could stay with them if I wanted, but I told him I doubted his mansion was handicap-friendly, so I'll probably hang out with you guys down here."

"We'd like that," she said as the van came to a stop nearby, its tall sides casting a shadow on the ground. A horse neighed in the distance. Even though she'd be gone. She'd never see Bryan again. Suddenly she felt like crying once more.

"You have any luggage?" said a black-suited driver who came around the back and pushed a button near a sliding door.

"Over there," Bryan answered, nodding with his chin to his cabin and the duffel bag Jayden spotted near the front door.

"I'll go get it."

"Stay," Bryan ordered, and then he smiled softly. "Let the man do his job. I wanted to talk to you anyway."

"Uh-oh," she said, watching as the driver headed off for the luggage, but not before starting the process of unfolding the device that would lift Bryan into the van, the whir of the motor filling the air.

"You love him, don't you?"

She didn't pretend not to know who he was talking about. "No."

Liar.

She gulped. "I care for him. I thought maybe one day there might be more, but it just didn't work out, and that's for the best. I've just begun my career as a therapist and I think I'm going to see if I can get certified or something to do hippotherapy because I really loved this job."

"Loved?"

She lifted her chin. Enough of this. "I actually turned in my notice."

A hand reached for hers, and it took her by surprise, and when she met Bryan's gaze, she could hide from herself no more. His eyes were like a rag that scrubbed the truth from her soul.

"He loves you, you know."

She shook her head vehemently. "Impossible." And there went her tears. And in front of Bryan Vance, of all people. "We barely know each other. Besides, if he loved me he wouldn't have left. But I guess it doesn't matter because now he's gone and by the time he gets back I'll be gone, too. Maybe. I don't know. But what does it matter?"

The newer, softer version of Bryan clasped her hand as tightly as he could, and she stared at the scars on his hands, aching for the pain he'd gone through in the same way she mourned her own broken heart.

"Don't quit."

"I have to."

"No, you don't." He used his other hand to roll his chair closer to her. "What he went through over there, Jayden, it had to be hell. I know. I went through much the same thing."

He shook his head, clenched her hand tighter.

"Things like that, they do things to you. Terrible things." His grip relaxed. "It can turn a charming and personable man into a nasty grump."

She had to wipe tears off her cheeks, took a deep breath and surprised herself by smiling. "You weren't that bad." Her stuffed-up nose made her sound like she had a cold.

"Don't give up on him, Jayden." Bryan's eyes filled with an intensity she couldn't look away from. "Don't quit. You're good at your job. Stay."

She bent and hugged him again. "Thank you, Bryan."

An arm came up and hugged her back, and she knew how hard Bryan had to work to lift that limb, and she felt a sob escape. Just one. That was all she would allow, pulling back to say, "I have a friend I want you to meet. Her name is Chandra. She's gorgeous and funny and a physical therapist, too, and she can be even more of a pain in the rear than me. I think you'd like her."

She thought he might say no, but to her surprise, he smiled a bit and said, "I'd like that."

One last hug and then a goodbye, and then she watched Bryan's van pull out.

Colby's truck drove toward her.

She stood there, frozen, and then the urge to run nearly overwhelmed her. He'd come back.

She loved him.

It hit her then, as she watched him drive toward her. Bryan had been right. Somehow, crazily, against all odds, she'd fallen in love with a man who didn't want her.

He pulled into the same spot where the van had just been, and she told herself to wave, to smile politely, to turn back to the barn and get to work. She didn't, though. Her feet were anchored to the ground by a deep and undeniable root of optimism that she hadn't even known existed.

The truck door opened. Her heart pounded. He slipped out. She couldn't breathe. He met her gaze, and her knees almost buckled. That was what it felt like. Like someone poked her in the crease of her legs so that her knees gave out, because there was a look on his face...

"Hello, Jayden."

She swallowed, clenched her hands. "Where have you been?"

He looked off in the distance, and she wondered if he would answer. Her heart kept time with every second that passed.

"I guess I was saying goodbye," he finally answered.

"To who?"

He shrugged. "One of the men I lost, but in a way, all of them."

And she knew what he'd done, knew by the look in his eyes that he'd found his peace in doing it. Knew, too, that Bryan had been right about one other thing. Colby loved her. She could see it in his eyes, hiding behind what remained of his sorrow.

"I can't even imagine," she said, her nose plugging yet again. Lord, she must look like a mess. Tearstained cheeks. Mussed hair. Probably dirt on her face, but she didn't care because Colby was walking toward her, and she felt a sob catch in her throat.

"I plan to visit them all. Every single grave, and meet with as many family members as I can."

She was nodding, although she didn't know what she was agreeing with. She just felt the need to say yes, to silently acknowledge, she supposed, that she approved of what he'd done.

"But there was one thing I couldn't say to my friend, Jayden. I said it once, but then I realized I was wrong, and that I didn't think it anymore."

He took a step toward her, so close now that she could have reached out and touched him, that she could smell him.

"I no longer wished it'd been me that'd died over there, and if you knew how often I've had that very thought over the past few years, Jayden, it would probably scare you. I used to think a dozen times a day that I should have been the one to die. I hid myself away…until you."

Her chest spasmed with a sob.

"Suddenly I had a reason to live. A motive for wanting to do better, for putting some good back into the world that had taken so much from me, and I'm not going to lie—it scared me."

She couldn't take it anymore. She closed the distance between them, and like she'd done so many times before, she leaned back, lifted a hand to the side of his face.

"I was scared, too." The tears ran freely down her cheeks now. She didn't care. "I was terrified of losing control. Of falling in love with you and having to completely redo my life."

His hand trembled. She saw it when he lifted it to her own face. "You don't have anything to worry about, Jayden. I'll take care of you. And I'll never leave you again. Never. I just hope that in time you'll learn to forgive me, and maybe even to love me back."

Silly, ridiculous, crazy man.

"Maybe?" she asked on a huff of laughter. "Don't you know, Colby? I *already* love you."

His eyes scanned her own, and she watched as the truth seeped into the crevices of his soul. Watched as his shoulders relaxed and his eyes grew soft and he realized that she was as much his as he was hers.

"I love you," he admitted.

She pulled his head down and they were kissing and she was crying and maybe he was crying, too, until a familiar voice said, "Now, *that's* what I call a reunion."

It was Jax, and he came toward them with Naomi, Tramp and Thor running up to them both, Tramp nearly knocking them off their feet. Derrick materialized from out of nowhere, too, the man grinning from ear to ear.

Jax came forward and shook Colby's hand, his "Welcome back" gruff with tears. And as Jayden looked around she knew she'd found forever friends, and that she and Colby were lucky to have them.

"Wait," Colby said a moment later. "I have one last thing to say."

Jayden saw him reach into his pocket, and her heart started racing all over again. He pulled out a tiny black box, and she knew what was inside, started crying once more, harder when he came toward her and knelt before her.

"Jayden Gillian, will you marry me?"

She didn't answer, couldn't have said yes if she'd tried—she was crying too hard. So she held out her hand, watching as he slipped a diamond ring on her finger, and then stood and kissed her once more, and she knew that somehow, miraculously, she'd found a forever love, too. And that it was a gift from above, their reward for all the heartache and the pain and the sorrow of the past, a love that would see them through good times and bad. A love that would last forever.

Epilogue

She would never, *ever* get used to Texas heat. Well, okay, not so much the heat as the dang humidity.

"Let me see," Patty said, the woman she'd hoped one day would be a coworker staring at her in approval.

Jayden pulled up her dress one last time, the heart-shaped neckline revealing a sheen of sweat on her breasts despite the air-conditioning that hummed in the background. They were in a dressing room, one with the sun beaming onto the floor, heat refracting off the surface. Oh, well. Nothing she could do about it. She turned and faced her friend. Brown eyes widened just before they went soft with love and approval.

"You look beautiful."

"Don't cry."

"I can't help it. You're like a fairy princess. And you're marrying a prince. Well, okay, Texas royalty, but it's damn near the same thing."

Was it? She supposed so. She and Paisley had been overwhelmed the first time they'd visited Colby's dad's. Paisley had walked inside the three-story mansion and said, "Mommy, is this a castle?"

Which had made her laugh and think that with its marble floors and Texas-sized backyard, it was just about.

She clutched the flowers Patty handed her, took a deep breath. In a few minutes she'd be getting married. She'd peeked out the windows earlier, at the backyard and the massive tent beneath which sat the crème de la crème of Texas. A few people in the crowd were her friends, plus Jax and Naomi and their kids. And more than a few were her family. But not her dad. She inhaled sharply. She'd invited him, had hoped…

"Are you ready to go down?" Patty asked.

Ridiculous. She should have known he wouldn't come. Reese Gillian was nothing if not stubborn.

She refused to cry. Preferred instead to focus on the present, and so she left the bedroom and headed downstairs. She'd never been one for big homes. They'd only agreed to hold the wedding in Texas for Colby's dad, a man who'd worked hard to try to make amends. They'd made progress. Slowly, but surely. The wedding today had been a huge concession on her part. She'd wanted to get married in Via Del Caballo, among friends and family, but something had told her to agree to a ceremony in Texas. It'd been the right thing to do, the planning having pushed her future husband and his dad closer together. She didn't know if Colby would ever fully forgive his father, but he might come close, and she wanted that, for Colby's sake and for the sake of their unborn children. That particular thought had her blushing, because tonight was the night. They'd made the decision early on to wait until they were married to consummate their marriage. She had no idea what Colby had planned for this evening, but she had a feeling she wouldn't get much sleep.

"You look beautiful, JayJay."

She stopped dead in her tracks.

Her dad stood at the foot of the stairs, tears in his eyes. "You didn't think I'd miss this, did you?"

Her shoulders started to shake, and she realized it was because she'd started to sob. He was here. He'd come. And then she was taking the remaining few steps two at a time, falling into her dad's arms as if they'd never been mad at each other.

"I'm so sorry, JayJay," he murmured in her ear. "I've been a stubborn ass."

She leaned back. "Yes, you have," she said, sucking in a breath and hoping like heck she hadn't ruined her makeup.

"Can you forgive your old man? Maybe let him walk you down the aisle?"

She saw it then, the sadness and the sorrow and the regret. And the tears. There were tears in Reese Gillian's eyes. It'd been so long since she'd seen him cry. "I wouldn't have it any other way."

"Let me see that makeup," Patty said. "Oh, dear. Hold on a moment."

They used tissue to repair the worst of the damage. Patty helped her pull a gauzy veil over her head, one that reached past the sleeveless gown that hugged her upper body and flared at the waist. Outside Aunt Crystal waited with Paisley, their four-year-old flower girl who was getting bigger every day and couldn't wait to watch her mommy get married in "the circus tent." Aunt Crystal smiled when she spotted her dad, and Jayden knew who she had to thank for getting him there.

"Thank you," she mouthed.

Crystal's eyes filled with tears. Jayden had to look away. She'd already ruined her makeup once today.

"Oh, Mommy, you look so pretty."

Coming from a four-year-old, it must be the truth, and so she smiled, but her lips trembled when she met Aunt Crystal's gaze.

"You look just like your mom."

The words robbed her of breath. How she wished her mom were here to see her today.

"Are you ready?" her dad asked, echoing Patty's words.

"Beyond ready."

And she was. She couldn't wait to get this over with. Couldn't wait to marry the man of her dreams, the man who'd been so remarkable with Paisley, who'd shown her through his actions the meaning of forgiveness and love and what it meant to give selflessly to others. He'd decided to use some of his trust fund money to open up a second Hooves for Heroes, this one located just down the road from his dad. They had officially turned over the care of Dark Horse Ranch to Derrick and Bryan. Yes, Bryan Vance, who'd moved to Via Del Caballo to be closer to Chandra, Jayden's schoolmate who'd taken her place, and to manage Hooves for Heroes with a little help from a few other veteran friends.

The sound of the wedding march rang out from the back patio. She'd descend a massive brick terrace into the garden proper, as Colby's dad called it, a place framed by rosebushes that released a fragrant scent into the air. Her dad let her go at the end of the aisle, and she smiled and leaned into him. Colby caught her gaze and glanced at her dad, and Jayden smiled. They'd have some catching up to do when all this was over, and she couldn't wait for her dad to meet her new husband.

Husband. Colby. That was what he'd be.

Her breath caught as she took his hand. He wore a tuxedo with cowboy boots, although he'd left the cowboy hat at home. He stood next to Jax, his best man, Patty taking her place opposite him across the aisle. And as she turned toward the minister she clutched his hand. He turned to look at her and mouthed, "You look beautiful," and she beamed.

The ceremony could have been spoken in gibberish for all she'd remember. All she knew was that she was marrying her love with her daughter standing beside her and family and friends who meant the world to her at her back.

So when the pastor said, "You may kiss the bride," she almost didn't realize what had been said. Only when Colby pulled back her veil, kissing her softly on the lips, did it finally register she was now Mrs. Jayden Kotch.

"Woo-hoo!" screamed her daughter, rose petals spilling out of her basket when she jumped up and down.

The audience broke into laughter and then applause, and Jayden felt like her face might split in half, she smiled so hard.

"You have a big night ahead of you, Mrs. Kotch," Colby said with a wag of his eyebrows.

"As do you, Mr. Kotch." She gave him a kiss, and then they were laughing, too, a sign of things to come. So much laughter and joy at their reception, and then later, when at last they became husband and wife in the truest sense of the word, more laughter, and tears, and a quiet joy in their hearts, a joy that would last.

* * * * *

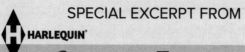
When Matt looked up, she offered him a shy smile. "Like I said, I'm sorry. I should have told you that you were a father."

"You've got that right."

"I've made mistakes, but Emily isn't one of them. She's a great kid. So for now, let's focus on her."

"All right." Matt uncrossed his arms and raked a hand through his hair. "But just for the record, I would've done anything in my power to take care of you and Emily."

"I know." And that was why she'd walked away from him. Matt would have stood up to her father, challenged his threat, only to be knocked to his knees—and worse.

No, leaving town and cutting all ties with Matt was the only thing she could've done to protect him.

HSEEXP0519

As she stood in the room where their daughter was conceived, as she studied the only man she'd ever loved, the memories crept up on her...the old feelings, too.

When she was sixteen, there'd been something about the fun-loving nineteen-year-old cowboy that had drawn her attention. And whatever it was continued to tug at her now. But she shook it off. Too many years had passed; too many tears had been shed.

Besides, an unwed single mother who was expecting another man's baby wouldn't stand a chance with a champion bull rider who had his choice of pretty cowgirls. And she'd best not forget that.

"Aw, hell," Matt said, as he ran a hand through his hair again and blew out a weary sigh. "Maybe you did Emily a favor by leaving when you did. Who knows what kind of father I would have made back then. Or even now."

Don't miss
The Cowboy's Secret Family *by Judy Duarte,*
available June 2019 wherever
Harlequin® Special Edition books and ebooks are sold.

www.Harlequin.com